A WEREWOLF IN SHEEP'S CLOTHING

BETTINA M. JOHNSON

Aqua Raven Publishing

A Werewolf in Sheep's Clothing

Copyright © 2021 by Bettina M. Johnson

Don't be a pirate. Nobody likes them unless they look like Will Turner rising in all his glory on The Flying Dutchmen. This book is licensed for your personal enjoyment only.
All rights reserved.
This book is a work of fiction. Any resemblance to persons living or dead, or places, events or locales is purely coincidental. (Stop being paranoid!)

ISBN: 978-1-7365176-9-7 (paperback)

Cover art by Tina Adams

❦ Created with Vellum

PROLOGUE

I hunger.

I can't control the urge to feed.

I've come to realize the monster within has all but taken over, and I have reached the point that I freely will surrender myself to it...

...to end the suffering. To gain the glory for my kind.

Oh! The agony of it all. The endless craving.

I wouldn't mind, not any longer, to fully embrace this evil. Not if it means I will have freedom again.

I can't control the beast, and it knows.

I pray those who cross my path meet a quick death and do not suffer as I have suffered.

But, then again, they are the hunted.

I am the hunter.

Their suffering would be different.

And I am well and truly lost because this excites me...the thought of their misery as my prey. This is why I am the monster among them. For they have no idea, my friends, that I have gone too far in my service...

To the beast within.
They have no idea the hunting will begin...
Yet.
But I'm coming for them.

CHAPTER 1

"I can't believe Johnny is upset with us. I mean, what's the big deal? So, we want to meet his family. We are well-behaved for the most part. Do you think he's embarrassed by us?" asked Bella while we maneuvered through traffic in Dallas, which meant I already had strained nerves.

"Maybe he's worried about them being an embarrassment to him. What if they all run around peeing on trees or chasing squirrels? That would be something to be embarrassed about, no?" asked Ellie, who hovered in the space between the two front seats of my Class C RV.

"Ladies, they're werewolves. I hardly think they remain in wolf form and chase squirrels," I responded.

"They might," sniffed Bella. She was cuddling Bob, my tuxedo cat, who was purring so loudly I could hear him over the traffic.

"He might be upset that we agreed to help his mother host a massive Halloween event...especially since he seems to be on the outs with his family," I said.

"Well, all I know is he's upset about something. And it has to do with his Texas relatives. Did you see how relieved he was when Dad couldn't get us out of our contract, and we had to wait until now to head to Texas? Here it is, October, and all that time wasted. We might never find that Ouija board now...it might be long gone!" Ellie grumped and swirled away in a puff of smoke.

Ellie is a ghost. She's also my sister.

I'm Maggie Fortune. Antique appraiser and monster-hunter extraordinaire. I'm the leader of an unnamed secret group of operatives who aid me in finding malevolent paranormal beings who would harm the human masses. We occasionally take out evil humans—anyone dark, evil, and so power-hungry they'd kill innocents.

No one on my team knows I'm their leader. It's a long story, but my dad is rich and powerful. His sister, my aunt, is the former leader of my group. So, the last thing I want is my team to think I got the job because I'm Daddy's little girl, and he has connections! Although lately, I believe some of my team might suspect there is more to me than meets the eye!

You're still stuck on the ghost comment, aren't you? OK, fine.

Ellie was turned into some kind of revenant by the man we are chasing. He performed dark magic on her, and now, from all outward appearances, she is a spook. However, we were informed by a few in the know, specifically a ghost-hunter and herself a revenant, that we can heal Ellie. However, she will always have extra ghostly tendencies. Once a revenant, always a revenant, I guess.

We're on the hunt for an item that may hold our next course of action or give us answers on how to cure Ellie. But right now, she is stuck and remains among us in all her ectoplasmic glory.

A few months ago, we received a lead that led us to a

man named Florin Vulpe—the very man who did the dark magic on Ellie. Thanks to a helpful Djinn named Barney, well, helpful once we liquored him up a bit and bound him so he couldn't escape, he gave us the name of this evil man. Now we are hoping to find a piece of a peculiar puzzle—one of the first Ouija boards ever made, a late 1800's model—which holds a map that leads to... well, we don't know what it leads to yet. But we have the key that opens it. So, I guess we'll find out if...no, *once,* we find it.

"I think Ellie is worried about that map, and Johnny is secondary. I mean, she's been moody ever since we found out about the Ouija board. I guess I would be too if I were in her situation."

"Yeah. Well, I want to know more about Johnny's family," said Bella with a wicked gleam in her eye. "I have a feeling there's a massive story there!"

"We will certainly find out about four hours or so from now—unless this traffic gets any worse. I still think it odd we've been invited to stay at their compound but not park close to where we're setting up."

"Maggie! You have got to be kidding me, right? We are staying on a large farm that borders Rocky Creek with big old pecan trees everywhere. If we feel like taking a hike, we can walk to our appraisal tents in 15 minutes by crossing the neighbor's property and Live Oak Street! It's only a three-minute drive!"

I frowned as yet another King Ranch pickup truck with a longhorn steer 6-foot horns tied to the front cut me off. It's not as if I could easily stop my 28-foot RV on a dime. I can't. "Well, I'm used to being right on site. I don't like making a habit of staying far from our tents."

"You just hate change. It freaks you out."

"Change hasn't been good to me. And what about Bob?"

"It was a funny movie?"

"Har, har. I mean my cat! I can't leave him parked in an RV across the street and a few acres away from where we will be working. What if my generator acts up, and he's locked away in a hot RV all day before I realize it? This is Texas...it's still warm in October! What if he gets out and wanders off on this farm and gets kicked by a mule? Johnny said his family has livestock of some kind...Bob will get trampled."

Bob, who'd jumped off Bella and chose that moment to cough up a giant hairball, didn't seem all that concerned.

"Are you kidding me? Bob spends all day asleep in your sink! He'll be fine."

We drove another hour before I heard from Antoine. "You there, Mags?"

"Roger."

"There's been a change in plans. Johnny's family moved us to a new location."

"Oh? Over?"

"Mags, you don't need to roger and over me. We're on a private line."

"I know. But I also know it drives you crazy, and you didn't stop Nathara from using one of her wishes to make me break out in zits. It took two weeks and a copious amount of medication from the arcane pharmacist to make them disappear."

I could hear Antoine sigh quietly and knew what was coming before he said anything. "Maggie... Nathara said she didn't use one of her three wishes on you."

"And you believe her?" I sulked.

"I have no cause not to," replied our somber vampire.

"OK, so my face spontaneously combusts in a magnificent eruption of pimples, and it's what? Hormones? I can tell you, Ant...it was *not* hormones. I'm twenty-eight, for heaven's sake! I haven't had pimples since I was sixteen!"

"Um, Antoine? Where are we staying now? If I don't ask, Maggie will spend another hour on the subject of those silly zits," asked Bella.

The traitor.

"We are going to be across the street at Johnny's personal property...also on Rocky Creek, but it backs where we're setting up and doing our thing. So it works out in the end."

I didn't know Johnny had personal property in Texas. Why didn't he mention it?

"And Johnny just informed you he has his own land?" I asked.

"It's complicated. I'll tell you more when we get there. It's on Live Oak, about ¼ mile from the old address I gave you. Just follow me, and we'll speak more when we arrive."

"Roger that!"

"You're a real pain sometimes, Mags."

"I live to please."

"Now I really want to know his family history!" cried Bella. "This is going to be an interesting two weeks!"

"Let's just hope it's an uneventful one."

I should have known better than to say that.

CHAPTER 2

Later that afternoon, we were all hanging around on lounge chairs behind our RVs, parked a short walk from the grounds that housed the antique show. The big rigs had arrived the day before, and I could see the workers setting up our tents in the distance. Our area—one that dealt in the more mystical artifacts that we kept separate from the main group's furniture, old books, vases, documents, and knick-knacks—was a short three hundred feet from where I parked my RV. That made me happy, especially since we were remaining in them to sleep at night. We'd all join Johnny in a big screened-in mess hall for our meals, kind of like a summer camp kitchen with picnic tables set up outside near the cooking area, all protected from the elements—and mosquitos!

The main building also housed indoor games and storage for the outside ones, the sporting equipment, and more bathrooms. Beyond that were two barns; one had farm equipment in it, the other seemed empty but at one time might have housed animals.

Johnny's property was vast, picturesque, and had only

one other building in sight. A log cabin in a clearing of trees a stone's throw from the creek.

The best part about where we were situated was the electric hookups and water stations we could tap into and the his and hers bathrooms attached to the mess hall. Johnny mumbled something about this being an old Boy Scout camp he purchased years ago, and it was RV-ready since they used it for camping.

"Oh! Volleyball. We haven't played since Charleston!" cried Sydney. Her sister Serena high fived her, and they went off in search of a ball.

"I've got to say. This place is wonderful. I couldn't have hoped for better."

"Which begs the question, why didn't old Johnny Boy offer it to us earlier? What's up with that?" asked Bella. "And where has he disappeared to?"

"Bella." Antoine chided the elemental, earning a scowl and monumental pout.

"I think something fishy is going on," said Nathara, "and you can try to warn me off and tell me to mind my business, but when Johnny's mother stopped by to say hello, he jumped up and grabbed her, dragging her away before we could even get to know her. What's up with that?"

"He's a private man, children...let him alone." Dara, our druid, scolded, although I could tell she was surprised by Johnny's behavior earlier as well. But Dara isn't one for gossip, so I'm not surprised she has taken the stance that we mind our business.

"OK, now that we've gotten everything sorted, I'd like to address something else," stated Antoine.

"What's up, boss?"

That I called Antoine "boss" was kind of an inside joke between him and me, all things considered. Antoine is my first in command, but to everyone else, the purported leader of our organization—my father's antique business being our cover. I say purported because I am the head of the entire United States division of the organization, as mentioned.

Antoine makes a stellar second in command. I couldn't ask for someone better suited to lead my team. Plus, he is a pretty intimidating-looking vampire—not that most humans could tell. But paranormals coming for appraisals behaved when they saw him hovering around.

I gladly handed him the "boss" duties because it was difficult enough dealing with my psychic powers and ghost-seeing expertise—not to mention I'm a pretty stellar witch if I say so myself. My psychic abilities are off the charts. My power intensifies tenfold if I touch something or someone, which makes for some interesting appraisals. I can handle an item and tell you who the past owners were, where it originated, and sometimes I will get whisked back in time and experience a vision so real it takes my breath away. I live in a pair of soft leather gloves. I rarely take them off, even in summer. Although, right now, I've switched to mesh ones with my fingertips poking out the top. I'm a highly sought-after appraiser in the paranormal world.

"We have an entire two weeks to investigate the whereabouts of that Ouija board, but in and among those duties will be your appraisals. Of course, everyone has their schedules, but does anyone have any questions?"

"I want to know why Sydney and Serena don't have to be here and are digging through the toys in the equipment room," snarked Nathara.

"Really, woman! That's all you can come up with? A complaint? Stop being so bitchy," cried Sven. He's a shifter and has the unique ability to turn himself into any object including his totem animal, and lately has been snipping back and forth with our dark witch. Nathara makes an easy target. Nothing ever seems to satisfy her, and she is often argumentative if only to play devil's advocate.

"Oh, sure. Pick on me. At least I'm here for this meeting and not playing with balls."

"There are so many responses I can give to that statement, but I think I'll pass...for now," said Sven.

Of all the paranormals on my team, Nathara is the most difficult.

"Nathara is still sore because she got stuck babysitting Barney, and he managed to slip away, embarrassing her. He showed us she can't manage one task without messing up," declared Sven as he slid his eyes over to Nathara to gauge how she'd react to that comment while arching his brow.

Nathara stood up, and I was half-convinced she'd lob some dark magic in his direction, but then to our utter horror, we watched as her face crumpled, and she began to sob, running for the RV she shared with Dara.

"Whoa. What was that about?" asked Tor. "Maybe someone should go see to her?" Glancing in my direction, I could only frown and shake my head slightly before he could volunteer me for the job. Nathara and I are frenemies at best. At our worst? Not, a good idea to go anywhere near her right now.

"I will check on her in a minute. Did you have anything else for us, Antoine?" asked Dara.

"We did cast a subtle ensnarement spell around the tents, right?"

We do this at every stop to set a trap that alerts us if and when someone, or something, truly evil crossed into our area.

"First thing," said Ellie.

"Well, I'm not expecting any trouble, but you never

know. Now, back to business. We will not go out willy-nilly to search for the Ouija board. I want a buddy system, and you can all stop groaning right now. Johnny told me this area is a hotbed of paranormal activity. Several Breed live in the area. All congregate for the Autumn Round Top antique events. The last thing we need is for something truly vile to wander in and we get caught with our guard down."

"But we've never had to employ a buddy system before, Ant. What is so different about this time?" I asked.

"This time, we have Johnny informing me that several of the old packs have begun pulling away from obeying the Order. I don't know what will happen if they go rogue. Let's hope it doesn't happen while we are here—but everyone needs to stay on their toes in the interim. Got it?"

We all assured Antoine that we'd be on our best behavior.

"Wait...do you mean like, um, wolf packs? Werewolf pack? What does it mean by them going rogue? asked Ellie.

"That's just it, El... we don't know. And for some reason, Johnny isn't forthcoming with an answer," said Antoine.

Oh really? Well, we will just see about that!

∼

The afternoon turned to evening, and the volleyball game was in full swing. Serena and Sydney were at it once again like they did in Charleston, all blonde hair and skimpy outfits. Quite frankly, I couldn't see the attraction of hitting a ball over a net, but then again, my idea of games had everyone sitting around a table doing trivia or playing cards. No one else seemed to mind them punting a ball back and forth over and over. Many enchanted males certainly appreciated the duos enthusiastic volleyball-playing antics.

While the game was going on, I went in search of our humble werewolf, who seemed to have disappeared. It didn't take me long, however. I found Johnny down by the creek—more like a stream, sitting on a tree stump.

"Maggie."

"Johnny. How goes it?"

I could see the movement that indicated Johnny let out some pent-up frustration by sighing. His shoulders dropped, and his head went along with it. Now he was contemplating the dirt at his feet.

"What do you want, Margaret."

Well, that was different. Never in all the years I've known my friend has he called me anything but Mags or Maggie. So, where did this formality come from, and what could it mean? After all, out of everyone in our group, Johnny was like my brother. Albeit one that shed and howled at the moon, but really, how many of you could say the same about your siblings?

"How about we start with you telling me why you have been so out of sorts these last few weeks? And now? Now you are downright morose! So, what gives, Johnny?"

"I don't want to be here. But I don't want to talk about it to you or anyone. Can't you people respect my wishes and drop it?"

I didn't know how to respond to this outburst which was so unlike Johnny. As a friend, I wanted to offer my shoulder and reassure him that we'd get through it together no matter the issue. But as the leader of this group, the boss in me knew I couldn't walk away and let Johnny have his privacy. This would be a delicate dance, however, because I didn't want to alienate him and cause a rift that might never get healed.

"Johnny, please talk to me. Whatever is troubling you might not sound so bad when you let in someone you trust. Don't I fit the bill? Perhaps it's not as bad as you think and only appears worse in your mind because you are bearing the brunt of it alone."

Johnny chewed on my words for a full minute, then turned to face me. I was shocked at how exhausted he appeared, and his eyes, red-rimmed and watchful, increased my concern up another level. Johnny looked like crap!

"We may have a rogue member in our pack...a renegade. My mother received a letter from the Order last week. Someone wrote to them accusing the pack of hiding an unstable renegade who hunts not only paranormal beings...but humans as well. My people are under investigation and have been for over a year, unbeknownst to us. Only, when questioned, no one in the pack knows who it might be—or is forthcoming with information. So, either someone is hiding this person, or they are adept at keeping their true nature hidden."

"OK. That's serious. But why shut us out? Why were you hesitant to come down here and to keep us from your family?"

Johnny stared at me in multi-levels of distress that had him finally shouting out, "Because most of my kin thinks it's me. Even my mother thinks I might be this renegade werewolf!"

That was the last thing I expected to hear!

CHAPTER 3

I found Tor heading in my direction early the following day. "We have a big problem."

"When do we not, lass?"

"Tor, I'm serious. I need to find Antoine, but somehow he slipped by us and is nowhere in camp," I said, wringing my hands. "Maybe he's over with the main appraisers checking on things, but I need to find him. Now."

Tor and I have finally come around to accepting we might possibly, could be at times, in a serious relationship. With each other even. Dating. Us.

We've been out to a quiet romantic dinner—finally— and now seem to be doing a weird dance of "what's next between us?" That we've known each other well over a year and had countless dinners with our group or solo when on a case notwithstanding, we finally got to go out on a proper date. We even exchanged a chaste kiss—on the lips.

Yes! On the lips, you heard me.

But we haven't had the time to sit and talk and discover things about each other. Nor do we know what to do about certain things about our, shall we say, individuality and character. That will be a hurdle to overcome. You see, I mentioned I'm a witch and a psychic. Tor, however, is a sorcerer—and a vampire. Yeah. Right there. That's the great big elephant in the room.

Tor, being a vamp, and a hot one to boot, all Scottish and manly and... ahem. I digress. He will outlive me. That's the short of it. I will live a long time. Witches can make it well into their three-hundredth year before riding off on that great broomstick in the sky. Vampires? Even three-quarter ones like Tor? Yeah...immortal. I haven't even broached the subject of his age yet. I've been too afraid. What if I'm dating someone who is five hundred years old?

Tor reached out and stopped me from continuing to run my hands through my hair by gently taking them and bringing them to his chest. "Come here."

I snuggled into him and breathed in his incredible woodsy scent.

Tor sighed. "What am I to do with you, lass? You take the weight of the world on sometimes—certainly when it comes to this operation and the people involved. Why is that?"

Here it is. The moment I have been dreading. Do I let Tor in on my secret? Should I tell him before we go in a direction hinting at commitment? Something a bit more intimate than we are now? I knew I didn't want him to keep secrets from me.

"Tor I...um...I don't know how to tell you this. I mean, I want to. I probably should have by now. It's just..."

"You don't want to let anyone know you are the head of our troop. The grand pooh-bah. Head honcho. Leader personified. How am I doing so far?"

A WEREWOLF IN SHEEP'S CLOTHING

I'm sure I looked like Daffy Duck when Bugs messed around and got Elmer Fudd to shoot his head off. Marching back with mouth agape and the inability to utter a word.

"You knew?! But how? When? I can't believe you've known...or guessed. How long have you known? Oh my gosh! Who *else* knows?" I was working myself up into a lather.

Instead of answering, Tor tilted my chin up and began to kiss me soundly. Like, open mouth, hello tongue, watch out for those fangs, soundly! I may have mewed a little. I certainly groaned. And I was more than disappointed when he ended the kiss and squeezed my shoulder. That was the longest and most intense kiss we'd ever shared. Where did that come from?

"I've guessed for a while now. Antoine verified it when I confronted him. It's not a big deal to me, Maggie. I'm not sure why you feel the need, although I can see why you would and will honor your wishes by keeping it a secret. But I have to tell you this," he said with a wicked gleam in his eye, "I'm looking forward to fraternizing with my boss."

"Oh, I hate to think of myself as your boss, but... wait. What?"

Instead of clarifying, Tor resumed his ministrations on my frazzled nerves by kissing me again, and we lost a good twenty minutes to kanoodling until Madame Myna came into the picture.

"Get a room! My word, in my day, two younglings would never be caught dead in a compromising position. Think of your reputation, my dear!"

Madame Myna is a seer who lives inside a crystal ball. She "belongs" to Dara, and most folks who visit her tent for appraisals think she's a Disney prop. Madame, not Dara.

Dara does not disabuse them of this notion and offers to do readings—for fun, of course.

I have no idea when her "time" was and assumed she is in the hundreds if not thousands as far as age goes.

"In your time, Myna, women were in harems and were told they should be seen and not heard," laughed Dara.

"And what's so wrong with that? Lying around all day, eating delicious food, painting your face, and combing your hair..."

"Having one man order you around and impregnate you with the other of his thirty wives and having to answer to his beck and call. Sounds lovely," finished Dara drolly.

"Well. There *is* that."

That begs the question. What is Madame? And how did she get into that crystal ball? Another mystery I needed to solve but never seemed to have the time to pursue. Although lately, I've been brushing up on all the various Breed in the paranormal world and what makes them tick.

"Enough of this nonsense. Maggie, we have a problem. Antoine is over in your tent with the main crew. It seems someone has dropped off an ancient-looking chest and the setup team found it near your table. Only, nothing is supposed to be in there right now."

I looked in alarm at Tor then back at Dara.

"It gets worse. Antoine tried to open it to see what's inside...and it growled at him."

"It what?"

"You heard me!"

This should be good. Well, at least we found Antoine.

～

"Why on earth would you call the police?" Antoine was standing in the middle of my tent scolding a terrified Sandy Booker and her sister Cassie, as principal event manager, Estelle Longo, worriedly looked on. Estelle worked directly for my dad and answered to him.

"I don't know! I heard there was a mystery chest, and then someone said it was growling. I didn't know if I should call the police or animal control, so I opted for the police!"

Antoine looked like he was about to implode, so I quickly stepped in and drew him aside.

"Antoine, she isn't aware of our situation. Neither of the Booker sisters knows about us. Cut her some slack. It's what's called for in any normal situation."

My words didn't seem to calm the ancient vampire down in the slightest. "And what do we do when they open that thing up and find...whatever the heck it is we'll find?"

"We are going to have to play it by ear when it happens. But we need to remain calm and appear as if we are just as surprised as the police when that lid comes off. Where are the police anyway?"

"They removed the chest to the far side of the field away from the crowd that formed. There have been many weird sightings, unexplained phenomena, and other oddities the good police lieutenant decided not to share with me. But something has been going on around here, and it looks like Johnny's family is involved."

Tor, Antoine, and I, heading in the direction of the last place the police said they'd be, found five officers, including the lieutenant standing around the ornate chest that they'd put a temporary barrier around. It looked like a tall dog run that was draped in a tarp to keep the looky-loos away.

"Who is in charge here?" asked the careworn lieutenant.

"I am," replied Antoine. "I introduced myself a few minutes ago."

"And you are?" he asked me gruffly.

"Maggie Fortune. My father owns this operation."

"Yet he's in charge. Why is that?"

Before I could respond with my practiced spiel, the lieutenant waved off my response and sighed. "Do you people deal in animals or something? You know animal trade is illegal, right?"

"It depends on the animal traded, but that's beside the point. We do not trade in anything living. We appraise antiques and buy and sell them. That's it, Lieutenant Foster." I scanned his name off the tag he wore on his shirt. He seemed surprised I knew what to call him until he glanced down at his shirt, frowning slightly.

This guy must be exhausted, he certainly looked it, and I figured between the antique festival and weird goings-on around town, he must be stretched thin.

"Well, if you hadn't noticed, that chest is engraved with tiny critters that look an awful lot like tiny foxes. The last thing I want is some rabid one to come rushing out and bite you all, so stand back."

The lieutenant went over to his men, and after a bit of prying and bashing of crowbars, we heard a distinctive crack, and the seal broke.

"OK, everybody, stay back. I think I've got this lid open," cried another police officer. We all moved away slightly but not far enough. We didn't have a good vantage point when they pried the lid off. It didn't escape my attention that the remaining officers drew their weapons, and I hoped whatever was inside didn't attack.

"Here goes!"

Bam! The lid popped off and toppled to one side while

A WEREWOLF IN SHEEP'S CLOTHING

we all craned our necks to see what sort of creature had growled. You can imagine our shock and dismay when curled up inside, frighten and filthy was one very pitiful-looking little girl.

This was not a good thing. Not by a long shot.

CHAPTER 4

The entire camp was crawling with police officers, and they even called in a few FBI agents. I had to quickly remove myself from the line of questioning and get in touch with our paranormal equivalent to the CIA... the Order of Origin. I needed some strings pulled, and I needed them in a hurry. Since I couldn't come forward as some obscure secret agent in homeland security or whatever agency would get seniority in this instance, I needed them to send someone to us who could override the local police and placate the Feds.

Imagine my surprise when Delvin Fitzwick, the Commander in Scotland and my superior, informed me I had someone in my troop who had those very credentials. Not only was I shocked, but I was also highly pissed off.

"Torquil MacDonald is assisting our group on an advisory basis, Lieutenant. We have an artifact we are hunting that may be on a local farm around these parts...at least that is where the last known sale shows it. It's a delicate matter, but he has his credentials in order and will assist you with any questions you may have." I uttered those words through gritted teeth when all I really wanted to do was kick Tor and Antoine because no way did that vamp not check out Tor's identity beforehand.

I didn't appreciate the head office going behind my back either. When this was all settled, heads would roll.

I had a famous temper, my red hair living up to its fabled reputation, and even Ellie swirled away to hide in my RV when I stomped off. Only I wasn't going to my RV. I marched over to the one Dara and Nathara shared, and I was spitting nails.

Of all the sneaky, underhanded lousy things to do to me. All this time. Ever since Tor had arrived as the newest member of our team, that lying scoundrel worked for the Order. He's probably my superior, and I've been under scrutiny, or my job is under review. I don't know why he's here, but those kisses we shared today were the last that man would ever get out of me, and you can put that in a pipe and smoke it!

And he had the nerve to say he liked me being the boss! *Hmpf.*

Opening the door with flair, I stormed inside the RV and confronted Nathara. "Why did you burst into tears like some pathetic middle-schooler who got her hair pulled by a bully?"

"What's up your behind, precious? Man trouble?"

I growled and slammed the door shut, then flopped on the sofa and pulled a toss pillow to my face. I don't think my screams carried all that far—not really.

"Whoa. If it is man trouble, I'd hate to see what Tor looks like about now," snickered Nathara. "What did he do? Accidentally sleep with someone?"

"I do not want you to mention that man's name in my presence. Do I make myself clear?"

"Loud and clear. Well, if you aren't here to talk about..."

"Arrgh!"

"To discuss any men... why are you here?"

"I told you," I replied snidely. "You started sobbing when Sven made that comment, and you and I both know you're made of sterner stuff. So, what gives?"

"What gives is we had a bit of an argument, and Nathara is vulnerable right now." Sven came walking out of the back of the RV, and his shirt was not only messy and wrinkled, but he was also hitching up his pants and tying his belt.

I stood there not registering what I was seeing—or trying not to anyway.

"I don't understand."

This was purely a tactical maneuver on my part since I most certainly comprehended what I was witnessing.

"Please. Stop pretending you're that naïve. After all, if you can get it on with Tor, Sven and I can do the same."

"But... but it's Sven!" Then, turning to Sven, I threw my hands in the air and pointed to Nathara. "That's Nathara!"

"Thank you for pointing out the obvious."

"But... that's not what I mean, and you know it! You and Nathara...but you *hate* her! You constantly complain about her antics. You...you..."

"She drives me to distraction, and I can't get enough of her."

For the second time in less than twenty-four hours, I remained motionless, mouth open, and was waiting for someone—anyone—to tell me I was in a bad dream. But then it dawned on me.

"You showed him! You pathetic hussy. Sven told me he could tell you were a shifter, but you probably did some dark witch kinky shifter magic and got all cozy with poor

A WEREWOLF IN SHEEP'S CLOTHING

Sven, and now he's under your thrall. You swished that little bird tail of yours and..."

"She showed me her most vulnerable side. Nathara released her Kestrel, and I was instantly smitten. We've been together since the first night we left Charleston. Months ago, now. Nathara was sad. I said something cruel to her today in front of you all, and we've since made up."

"And by together, I assume..."

"You assume correctly."

"And now you made up?"

"Precisely."

Well, how do you like that? No wonder she's been ignoring me lately. Nathara has been otherwise occupied—and with another shifter to boot!

I worked my jaw back and forth, not happy with this situation one bit. Probably more to do with the fact that Tor and I were officially over, and I didn't want to see anyone else deliriously happy—and these two were freaking glowing!

"A snow leopard and a Kestrel. How's that working out for you? Does he forget himself and chase you around the woods trying in vain to make you a tasty snack? Does he sneak up on you and pounce, knocking off a few feathers before you fly out of his reach?"

Nathara didn't deem it necessary to respond, rolling her eyes and giving me a bland look instead.

I faced her and continued my tirade. "What? Do you often change his litter box if you keep him sequestered away in here too long without a nighttime potty break? Where is Dara staying anyway? Isn't this her RV?"

I knew I had my snark dialed on high, but I couldn't help it. I also acknowledged this has more to do with Tor being a secret agent of the Order—more secret an agent than the rest of us, that is—and I needed to focus my anger on something—or someone else. Nathara was my intended target, but suddenly I felt the need to lash into a man.

"And you...so much older than Nathara. Taking advantage of a young witch, are you? You should be ashamed of yourself!"

"Maggie, please stop. I know why you're upset. I just got off the phone with Antoine. He told me about Tor being undercover," Sven murmured.

"He's what? What do you mean?" cried Nathara.

"Tor is a highly-skilled assassin and higher-up in The Order of Origin. He outranks everyone in our organization by far."

"Oh! That explains so much. Maggie here is upset because she likes being Antoine's second in command...and now that rank goes to Tor. Or is he even higher than Antoine?"

"I would watch how I speak to your superior, Nathara. For your information, I am your boss. Antoine works for me. And as for Tor, he can try to outrank me, but he will have to fight me first."

And with that, I slammed out of the trailer and marched over to Johnny's cabin, hoping I'd find him inside because I needed a friend.

Belatedly I realized I'd let the cat out of the bag, and now everyone would know I was in charge. Then how come I felt like a recalcitrant teenager and not the leader of our group?

Probably because I looked the fool, flying off the handle and showing I couldn't control myself—or my legendary temper.

What an infernal mess!

However, before I could reach the cabin, Sydney came

running across the field, waving her arms, and calling out to me. I stopped and turned, waiting to see what manner of mischief she would inform me had befallen us now.

"Maggie, come quickly." Ellie came swirling out of the darkness to grab my arm and tug me toward the main camp.

"Not now, Ellie. I'm tired, and I've had enough drama for one day."

"Well, too bad. We have a bigger problem than your bad mood and need for sulking."

Whoa. Ellie is firmly on team Maggie. My sister never calls me out when my temper gets the better of me, and I drew back, pulling my hand free from her grasp. Yes, she's a ghost. And yes, Ellie can manipulate matter... well, my matter. Despite her condition, she's always been able to touch me. Go figure.

"What on earth is the matter now?"

"That little girl. They brought her to the police station and called Child Protection Services to get her, but she managed to escape when they arrived at the police station! So she's out there somewhere, and we need to find her."

"We need to find her, Ellie...and we need you to go on the offensive." I began to rub my forehead, my headache letting me know it was about to get serious. "I think this case is going to call for your special talent. Round up all the cops that were here today...and turn your suggestion powers on. Make them forget this kid existed...or we are going to have news teams down here by morning."

Time for all hands on deck.

CHAPTER 5

"What are we doing wandering around the woods behind the police station and courthouse at 3:00 AM anyway?" Bella asked me the next day. Well, early morning on the same night but only a few hours from daylight. No one sneaking around at 3:00 AM was up to any good.

"Because Johnny needs that little girl not to be taken in by Child Protection Services. He said right off he could tell she's a wolf cub—his words. We know that means she's a werewolf and a feral one at that. So until Ellie finds every single officer and those federal agents, we need to make sure we get hold of her her first."

"But why us? I understand about all that. I was there at our meeting. I just wondered why you and I were tasked to stake out the municipal building and no one else."

Yeah. Why were we the ones who were sent on this midnight reconnaissance, anyway? Everyone else was scouring the wooded area near our campground, figuring that maybe the child would head back to where they dropped the crate off.

I would undoubtedly run far away from authority

figures if I were a frightened child. I doubt she'd be hanging around here.

"Perhaps it's because of your innate ability to morph into a room and snoop around, and my stellar psychic skills that can warn you if I sense anyone is afoot?"

"Maybe. Or maybe it's because Tor has been trying to get a word in edgewise with you, not to mention some alone time, and he's over there as we speak hovering on that rooftop. Do you think he asked Antoine to send you here so he can have a word with you?" Bella pointed with her chin, smirking a little.

"I refuse to speak to him, and you better have not set this little rendezvous up, Bella, or I will make you pay." Especially since the second I looked to where Bella pointed, Tor mysteriously vanished. He probably turned into a bat and flew off—the big jerk. But if Bella continued to goad me, I'd flog her!

Yeah, right. Like I could do anything genuinely horrid to an earth elemental. Bella could turn the ground into two massive boulders and smush me between them before I could even think of clicking on my witchy magic. I'd be an old crone pancake faster than you could say, "hocus-pocus."

"You jest. First of all, I don't have it in me to play games and set up a rendezvous. Second, I don't think Antoine would either. I think maybe Tor is here because he likes keeping an eye out for you. that, and vamps see well in the dark. Look, Mags...just let him explain. It's not like you have the right to point fingers. Look what you've kept from us all! You're my freakin' boss! If anyone should be upset, it should be the collective crew, but we haven't got our panties all wadded up about this new turn of events. Why can't you offer the same courtesy to Tor?"

Why indeed?

Changing the subject, I went to someplace from which I was sure Bella couldn't be distracted. "And what do you think about Dara shacking up with Antoine? With Nathara having her talons in Sven? He moved in with her, and Dara got kicked to the curb, so Antoine took her in. You don't think...?"

"That those two ancients are getting it on? They're both around the same age—give or take five hundred years. Who knows?" Bella replied. "What's that?"

"What? Where?"

"Over there by the dumpsters! Is that? Oh, my word! It's the child! She did stay close to the police station. I hope she doesn't run off when she sees us!"

And just like that, our night became even more interesting.

~

"Ow! You little beast! Bite me one more time, and I'll shave your head!"

"I don't think you should threaten a little girl, Mags. She's what? Eight? The poor thing..."

"The poor thing had better have gotten her rabies shot, or I'm going to start frothing at the mouth soon."

"Grrr."

That was the only sound we'd managed to get out of the tiny werewolf. After that, I wasn't sure if she understood us or not, and any attempts at communication got us growled at or bitten.

We spent the rest of the early morning chasing that little brat hither and yon while she remained just out of reach. Then finally, the sun rose, and we trudged through woods and fields hot in pursuit, and Bella and I even managed to cross a rather substantial stream only to find the little monster had circled back to the other side before climbing a large sycamore tree.

"Who's climbing up there to get her down?" Bella asked.

"I have no intention of going up any tree to get a rabid wolf cub. She's a monster."

"She's a little kid, Mags! How about you use magic?"

"And what? Blow her out of there? I have half a mind to do it."

"I don't know. I can make a small earthquake happen and shake her out, maybe."

"Oh, that will go over well with the locals. How many earthquakes happen in the Texas hill country?" I grumbled.

"I can keep it small and localized."

That's how we managed to nab the varmint, uh...child.

Ellie spent all morning hunting police officers. I tasked her to start from the top and go down, wiping the memory of all the cops who were present for the big reveal and make them think the incident was a Halloween prank. Halloween was only days away, and it fit the narrative. Unfortunately, many officers called their girlfriends and wives to give them the inside scoop on the 'little growling girl.' Still, after an hour of ghosting them around—pun intended—she'd managed to get to everyone—including the Feds. I'd just hung up the phone with Dara, who informed me Ellie was back in camp.

I let her know we had the child and would meet everyone there in a few minutes.

Well... had was a matter of opinion. We had the child cornered, but every time we reached out to take hold of her, she'd go into a fit of rage and start snapping at us.

"OK, listen, kid. We are trying to help you. Don't you

understand us? Help? See? I'm smiling! If I was going to hurt you, why would I be smiling?"

"I feel like hurting her, and that makes me want to smile." Unfortunately, Bella was not very helpful.

"We need a muzzle and a leash," I grumbled.

"Or a newspaper!" laughed Bella.

Instantly the little girl became still. She recoiled and began to whimper softly.

"Hey! Hey...no, Bella was kidding. We won't hit you, honey. I promise." Looking at Bella, who shrugged, equally not knowing what we were dealing with, I tentatively reached out and proceeded to put my arm around the little girl guiding her over to my Jeep, which I'd hidden behind a donut shop. Got to love it. We chased the girl all over the town from the police station into the woods, through a field, and into a tree, only to have her drop to the ground and head back to the police station where we cornered her behind the donut shop.

My head was still reeling with the idea of the police station being directly across from a donut shop. I guess it's convenient, and it explains the girth of the majority of the policemen we'd seen so far. Except for one tall, thin, and mean-looking policewoman who had the harried appearance of someone who was at the end of her rope. She was posted at our campground all night and looked like she couldn't wait for her shift to be over.

Who could blame her? All she was supposed to do was watch us and the compound, and we collectively gave her the slip.

Ellie wiped her mind clean of this as well.

It was great having a sister who could influence and suggest things so humans didn't remember interacting with us. The ghost thing, not so much.

The little girl stopped fighting us and followed along quietly as we came upon my Jeep. Once settled inside, I turned to give her another reassuring grin, and she responded by glowering at me with a slight snarl.

"I don't think she likes you very much," chuckled Bella.

I just sighed and pointed the vehicle back in the direction of the campground.

It didn't take us very long to get there. Round Top isn't a large town, and I noticed right away that something was going on over by the far end of the property where we were parked, which butted the event area near our tents.

"Why is everything all lit up?"

"Maybe it's a welcoming party for the little werewolf?" Bella suggested.

"I don't know. Everyone seems to be scrambling around looking for something."

"Well, we'll find out in short order. I wonder if Tor is back yet."

I wondered that as well and knew I needed to confront him about this new situation sooner rather than later. I also needed to understand why he was spying on us from the courthouse roof. Did he not think I could handle things on my own? And when did he disappear? If he was spying on us, didn't he see us go on a wild goose, uh, wolf chase after that kid?

I didn't enjoy the way my stomach did nausea-inducing flips-flops at the thought Tor might think me inferior in my duties. Nor did I like the way I became pathetically needy, wanting him to believe I could handle anything that came my way. I don't need Torquin MacDonald's praise! I don't!

It has nothing to do with the fact that my mother died young and my current strained relationship with my father, thank you. I'm an adult, and I do not need to seek out attention or approval from anyone.

Much.

We came to a stop, and I gave the child another reassuring grin before opening my door and hoping for the best. The best is that she didn't run off the second we let her out of the Jeep. Instead, Bella hopped out, opening the door for the little girl who tentatively exited my vehicle immediately latching onto Bella's hand.

She couldn't be so accommodating when we first found her? And now suddenly, Bella is her savior? Fine. Be that way.

"What's going on?" I asked Dara who clutched Madame Myna in one hand and held her palm to her forehead with her other hand.

"There's been an incident of sorts. Well...something happened and... well, no. I wouldn't say it happened. But something did it, so...oh, I don't know how to explain!"

Do you think?

"Dara. Take a deep breath and tell me what occurred here while we were gone."

"Oh! You did find the child. Is she faring well, do you think? Has she spoken yet?"

"Dara! What happened this morning?" I was beyond exasperated at this point and knew I shouldn't yell, but I felt the tingling of a migraine coming on.

"I'm sorry! I must sound the fool. Someone, or something, rather, tossed the tent area, knocked a few chairs over and ripped the canvas, leaving a gruesome present for us to discover when we investigated."

"Gruesome? What did you find?"

"Well, the consensus is that the poor creature at one

time was a possum...but now it's a bloody mess. Sorry to be so graphic."

"Was it a coyote? Or some other creature that hunts? Maybe it dropped its meal and became disoriented?"

"Oh....no, no. It couldn't be an animal. On the contrary, Sven thinks it might be something with evil intent. For, you see, our alarms went off. Moreover, the possum was intact, except something removed all of its skin."

Oh, ick. I didn't like the sound of that.

What new horror are we dealing with this time?

CHAPTER 6

After a harrowing few hours scouring the campground for whatever might have left that wretched possum for us to discover and coming up empty-handed, we settled the little girl in with Johnny's mother. She finally introduced herself to us, despite him doing everything in his power to keep his family at bay.

"She will get a good solid meal, and we'll clean her up. Maybe then she will feel like talking and can offer us an explanation as to how she wound up in that trunk, who put her there, and who her pack is."

Cutting a scathing look to Johnny, Charity Baldoni seemed to infer it might be her son who needed looking into. I found the lack of warmth between mother and son disconcerting. Charity had been nothing but a gracious hostess to us. But I knew I needed to find out why there was this animosity between them.

Johnny meant a lot to me, and I felt I owed him to get the story straight. Especially since I knew werewolves were a tight-knit pack, and something pretty appalling had to have happened to cause this mistrust between mother and son.

The rest of the afternoon into evening didn't garner any answers. We didn't find anything in the way of tracks, and we didn't find any blood trail. The strange thing is our alarm that detects evil kept going off randomly as if it could still sense the presence of something in the area. So, we finally nullified it, if only to get some sleep! Sven offered to keep watch for the night, and Sydney said she'd relieve him if and when he needed it.

The following day found most of us preparing for a day appraising antiques while the other half decorated the camping sight with Halloween decorations. We would be hosting a massive party on the big night and the week leading up to it: hayrides, pumpkin chucking, ghost tales around the campfire. Several families in the area were coming, and we expected quite the crowd. Johnny's family always did it up big for the town and surrounding area, which would be no exception this year.

I worried about the validity of holding a Halloween party with some unknown creature among us, but when everyone voiced their displeasure as soon as I suggested we cancel, I backed down.

Don't come blaming me if someone's tiny ghoul or ghostly trick-or-treater gets snatched by the bogeyman, then!

All of us were planning to don costumes and get into the spirit of the holiday, but now I had my hands full, literally, with old creepy dolls and a few doll heads. The woman who entered my tent specifically asked for me, and I was confused because I didn't deal in old dolls. Maybe a stray voodoo doll or some possessed puppets, but baby dolls and Barbies? No, thank you.

The woman carried herself like royalty and had silver hair, a slim model-like stature, and molten brown eyes that seemed to have a flame dancing in them. She introduced herself as Francine Adolpha.

"I think this one is the Baby Tears doll from the P&M Doll Company in New York. P&M stands for Paula Mae. They used to be quite a large company on Wooster Avenue and are famous for their dolls with blinking eyes and pretty faces compared to some. I think she is circa 1957...but I'm not a doll expert. If you want, I can point you to..."

"No. That's not necessary. I didn't come here to show you all my dolls. I'm taking them to one of the big consignment shops here in Round Top. I came to show you this."

Immediately I sensed something wrong with the tiny doll the woman thrust out at me, and I recoiled rather than touch it. I had on my gloves, due to my photoscopic and retrocognitive psychic abilities. I didn't want to risk it. I certainly wanted to remain here in the present, thanks! You can imagine how disorienting it would be to inadvertently touch something and go bye-bye when I least expected it. Nevertheless, this talent made me highly sought out and somehow this woman had heard about me.

"That's an Eskimo doll, possibly from the 1930s. But something is off about it...can I ask you where you found it?" I was shivering and must have given a signal to Bella because she suddenly materialized by my side even though she didn't have any customers slated for today.

"That's creepy," sniffed Bella.

Francine didn't seem offended by our observations but looked keenly at Bella then me like we passed her test.

"You're famous, of course, Miss Fortune, and I knew I had to come here today to see what reading you'd get off this doll. I live a few miles away; Charity Baldoni can vouch for me. We are neighbors. I heard about your talents—you *are* famous in our world."

See?

OK. So, Francine is paranormal. It's not as easy as one would think to tell the various Breed, but her knowledge of me ended any question of this. I just wondered if she was a witch or werewolf.

"You'd like me to touch it with my bare hands. Is that what you're inferring?"

"Yes. Please. I need to know...well, I need to know something specific about this doll. Can you do this for me?"

"I can, but my price just tripled. I'm sorry, but this item is giving me the heebie-jeebies, and touching it will be akin to some form of torture, I'm sure."

"Of course! Anything. I will pay whatever price you ask of me."

OK, then. This day just became ten times more interesting.

"Bella, can you get Dara in here and find Serena or Sydney. I want them to guard the entrance to my tent. I don't want anyone else wandering in while I do this. I have a feeling it's going to be a bumpy trip for me—if you know what I mean."

Bella ran off to do what I asked, and I offered the woman a seat.

"Can you tell me anything about this doll before the others get here?" I asked.

"I'd rather not say too much. Other than we locked it away in my family vault for years, and when my mother passed away, I was finally allowed to remove it. It's been a debatable item and has a bad history in my family. It caused a rift among my people, which still hasn't healed. Someone crafted the doll in Canada in the late 1920s, so you were close in estimation, but when my mother received it as a child, all manner of horrible things befell our pack, and they wrapped it up and put it away under lock and key."

Pack? Werewolf, then.

"Why did your family not get rid of it or bring it back to the artisan who made it?"

"Superstition, I suppose. It was made specifically for my family by an old witch. I don't know the full story, but needless to say, no one wanted to insult the witch by returning it to her."

Indeed.

When Bella returned, I was upset to find Tor on her heels and almost barked something at him, but then thought better of it. Not in front of clients...but later we were going to have words. Dara came to stand by me with a bag of her cleric medicinals in case I needed something when I came back.

"I'm going to take my gloves off now and will touch this Eskimo doll. Would you please refrain from touching me even if I moan or thrash about? I am in no danger. But sometimes, it appears that I am. This shouldn't take long."

Slipping the gloves from my hand, I reached out and plucked the doll up off the table.

And I found myself in the bowels of hell.

༄

Women screaming and a baby shrieking were the first things to register. Then I smelled the blood and could hear something dying close by, gurgling and wheezing. There was a lot of fire and smoke, and the stench of burned flesh made my stomach lurch.

Blinking rapidly, I allowed my eyes to adjust to the

vision that felt all too real, then gasped at the devastation in front of me.

A small village was burning. Bodies lay strewn about the area, most of them in a bloody heap. At my feet was a large grey wolf—bigger than any wolf had the right—bleeding and in tremendous pain. It sported a ghastly wound, yet it was still alive.

Instantly, I knew I was the person who struck the fatal blow to the poor creature. I was inside, looking outward.

Much to my disgust and shock, the person reached out, and using a sharp knife, took hold of the wolf and began to skin it alive. The helpless creature screamed in pain, and I almost passed out from the depravity of it all. Finally, when this evil person was satisfied with the amount of fur skinned from the dying wolf, they leaned down and whispered something in a strange language...and I tried to remember every word even as I was whisked back to the present day.

"Nu dør du, ulv. Og din magt bliver min," I uttered, then toppled out of my chair and onto the grass below.

"What is she saying? What does that mean? Is that German?" cried Bella in alarm.

"No. That is Danish. It means, 'now you die, wolf.' And your power becomes mine," said Francine with a shudder. "This is worse than I expected."

Tor came to my rescue and had me propped up in his arms. I was too weak to swat him away like an annoying and unwanted gnat infestation. The look of concern on his face almost thawed me out a little, but he didn't comprehend, fully, the wrath of the red-headed me. I had no intention of making this easy on him.

After taking a long sip of water laced with some tincture from Dara, I returned to my seat and faced the woman.

"What do you mean, worse than you expected? I haven't even told you what I saw yet."

"What did you see, my dear?" she asked.

"Someone... some horrid, evil person was sitting in the burning village with bodies everywhere, all charred and smoking. And lying at their feet was a massive dark grey wolf...or, um...wolf. This person took a nasty-looking knife and skinned the poor animal alive!"

Francine gasped at this and appeared frightened at the same time. "Please go on."

"That's it. The wolf was still alive when I morphed back to you, but I heard those words before I returned. I can't tell you if it was a man or woman who did this to the poor animal."

Francine looked down, and I noticed a few teardrops falling onto her clasped hands. Then she faced me once more with fire in her eyes. "That was no animal. That was my ancestor...a werewolf. This doll was made from the fur stolen from him that day. It's cursed!"

Oh, well, that explains the heebie-jeebies I felt earlier. I always manage to get the genuinely messed-up cases.

Lucky me.

CHAPTER 7

"Boy, do you manage to get some pretty freaky cases." Nathara was sitting across from me, dining on fried chicken, collard greens, and creamy, cheesy grits, thanks to Charity, who'd shown up with her pack and an overabundance of food. I gave Nathara a stern look and poked at my meal. My appetite, compromised by what I saw in the vision, hadn't returned as of yet.

"Just last week you had that haunted necklace to deal with...so don't give me grief."

"Like a haunted necklace is anything compared to a cursed Eskimo doll covered in the fur of someone's relative. That has got to top anything you've had in ages," sniffed Nathara in reply.

"Yeah, well, I didn't appreciate your angry poltergeist running amok in Greenville, so shut it."

Nathara rolled her eyes and took another healthy bite of chicken. "My poltergeist was nothing more than a pissed off teenager who didn't like that she had died. It meant she'd missed the homecoming dance, and she was supposed to be queen."

"She shouldn't have taken those drugs then drank herself silly, or she'd still be among the living. It took forever to get her to accept that she'd passed. And what a mess that was! We need a Geisterjäger like that Samantha chick we met when visiting my cousin Lily in Sweet Briar, Georgia. She'd have gotten that girl to depart this world posthaste."

"Yes, well, instead, we had to perform that miserable ritual together, and that's a bonding experience I could have done without," grumped Nathara.

You and me both, sister.

"So, Francine is a werewolf and some kind of kin to Johnny in a roundabout way?" asked Dara, who was making herself a plate.

"That's what she told me," I responded.

Just then, Tor came over to where we were dining and took the seat next to me. He reached over and grabbed a chicken leg off my plate.

Now it was me who was growling.

"Hey. You're not eating, and I'm starved, lass."

I didn't bother giving a response.

It wouldn't have been proper. Not with a child present.

The little girl still hadn't spoken a word but was currently eating double her body weight in chicken and potato salad. She was making tiny, happy noises while she tore the meat from the bone, and it made me squeamish all over again.

"Antoine thinks we have some kind of rogue werewolf causing trouble. And no, he doesn't believe Johnny has anything to do with it. First of all, it's Johnny! And second, he's been with us constantly, and one of us would have seen him slip away and such. Since he's not taken any vacations lately, we've concluded he must have done something to upset his family and makes a good scapegoat taking the heat off themselves."

"What? You think one of Johnny's relatives is guilty of whatever is going on?"

"Antoine and I don't know what to think," replied Tor.

Oh, so now it was Antoine and Tor having weighted discussions about group matters. Great.

"And where did you disappear to? Or did you think I hadn't spied you skulking around like a typical vamp?" I scolded.

"I saw that policewoman rushing away from the station and went to investigate. I thought it odd that she'd be there so early in the morning and with the child missing, I thought it prudent to check it out. When I caught up to her, she claimed she was looking for our escapee. I didn't see any reason to continue questioning her and figured Ellie could work her magic on her later in the day, so I let her be on her way."

I ground my teeth then returned to poking my food around my plate. "She didn't seem suspicious to you?"

"No. Just concerned and doing her job. She is a police officer after all."

"Seems convenient if you ask me."

"Perhaps. Or perhaps she truly just wanted to help. However, Antoine is trying to figure out what to do about this odd situation and what to tell the Order.

"That's right. I'm perplexed by this incident. And we need to put our heads together and figure out what we know so far," said Antoine, who took the seat next to Nathara and gave me a long, weighted look. "What are your thoughts, Mags?"

Now he wants my opinion. Perhaps Tor's ideas fell short...or maybe the two of them wanted to see what I'd come up with and decide on my worth. Not that Antoine had any say. I am the boss, damn it!

Then start acting like it, Maggie. I berated myself.

"I don't think this is the work of a werewolf at all."

Charity Baldoni had just come over with a pitcher of iced tea to refill everyone's cups and jerked her head in my direction. "Why not? What do you suspect?"

Taking the empty seat on the other side of Antoine, she placed her elbows on the table and stared at me with rapt attention. It didn't slip my notice that Johnny, who was on his way over to grab a bite to eat, veered away from us. He sat at another table.

I had thoughts ruminating around my mind and kept trying to piece together these incidents, which I couldn't see as anything but connected. But in what way, I still had no idea.

"Before I answer that, Charity, I need you to explain something to me. I'm not trying to be rude, but you have to understand, Johnny is like a brother. I adore him. It's come to my attention that you suspect him, your son, of being guilty of whatever it is we are dealing with now. I need to know why."

If Charity seemed upset with my putting her on the spot, she didn't show it. Instead, she looked resigned and offered her explanation simply and without much drama.

"Johnny is not my biological son. His father and I met and married after Johnny's mother passed away rather young, from cancer. He barely remembers her, and I've been the only mother he's known." Charity paused and peered over to where Johnny sat entirely alone and sighed.

"When Johnny was a young teenager, he did something that made him a virtual outcast in our pack."

Unable to grasp what Johnny could have possibly done

that was so horrible to cause his rift with the pack, I suddenly became uneasy and hoped my opinion of my dear friend wouldn't alter once I heard what Charity revealed.

"He never got along with my son, Benji. Benji was my eldest and looked exactly like his father, my spouse, who died in a car accident two years before I met Giovanni Baldoni, Johnny's dad. Johnny was upset when his father adopted Benji, effectively making him the firstborn male in this pack. Although we tried to assure Johnny he was the rightful next in line to command Johnny and Benji...well, Benji could goad and tease. I believe he taunted Johnny, making him think Giovanni had secretly appointed him to second, effectively handing him the role as his successor.

"One day, both boys were out in charge of sheep duty. As you can see, this area of Texas has quite the sheep farming operation going over the traditional cattle. Our family is no different. We have a huge flock. Anyway, the boys were out mending fences and counting the flock when a fight broke out. Johnny, to this day, refuses to say why they argued. But one thing led to another, and both boys transformed into their wolves and began to fight."

Charity paused here and gazed down at her hands gripping the table. We'd all gasped upon hearing this news, knowing the penalty was swift and fierce for those werewolves who would turn and attack another in their pack. Even in polite society, werewolves were forbidden these days by the Order from settling arguments by transforming into their baser selves. Charity's knuckles were white with the tight strain as she held her hands together. She tightly clasped them in her lap, possibly to stop them from trembling, which was evident in her voice when she continued her story.

"Even though Benji was the elder of the two, he was a

slight young man, short for his age and rather delicate. Johnny was much bigger and... well, look at him. He's very fit and strong. Even at fourteen, Johnny was something to behold. We don't know if something snapped in him or if he felt threatened by Benji...we don't know what caused him to become so fierce. Despite Giovanni becoming aware of the brutal fight and rushed to intercede, Johnny had grasped Benji by the throat."

Charity began to cry softly, gentle tears slipping from her eyes and streaming down her face. "Benji was dead by the time Giovanni reached him, and Johnny ran off and didn't come home until a neighboring pack found him hiding in one of their grain barns five days later."

"And all this time, Johnny never said anything? Never defended himself?" cried Nathara, who seemed highly agitated, unusual for her since she always remained calm whenever confronted by horrible news.

"Johnny only spoke of this once, at a tribal council to decide what should be done with him. He stated Benji had become bewitched by an older woman and became her lover. She had him under some kind of enchantment, and he was plotting the death of Giovanni so he could ascend to pack leader." Charity glanced at us all before casting her eyes once more in Johnny's direction.

I could feel my team follow her gaze and became chilled, realizing I sensed a collective pulling away from Johnny. As if everyone present could find him at fault and already became judge, jury, and executioner. What's more, from the shocked expression on Johnny's face as he jerked his head up and turned our way, I could tell he knew we knew.

I offered him a reassuring smile, but he dropped his head down dejectedly and pushed his plate away.

A WEREWOLF IN SHEEP'S CLOTHING

"The only reason he's free today is because of Giovanni. He refused to let his only son be put to death and pardoned him despite not believing this wild tale. Ever since, Johnny has been a pariah in our community...but because he is his father's son, we defer to his will that Johnny is not shunned—or worse. However, my youngest son, Derek, is now the pack leader—Giovanni died a few years back. So, Johnny has no position, and he is forbidden to mate...have a wife and children, at least among the werewolves—we don't care if he weds out of Breed. We need to protect our kind after all. So, there you have it."

"And you don't believe a word of what Johnny claimed?" I asked.

"I don't know what to believe! You have to understand that even though Johnny is not my flesh and blood, I loved that little boy as if he were my own and raised him to be his father's son. But Benji...he was my firstborn. A mother doesn't get over something like what happened, let alone at the hands of one she raised. I don't know what to think."

"And now, with this new mystery going on...you and the pack fear it might be Johnny's doing because who else would it be? Is that right?" Antoine probed, resting his hand gently on Charity's.

"I do. We all do. Johnny has never shown any remorse for what he did to Benji. Furthermore, if you press him to this day, he insists my boy was a monster in disguise. A wolf in sheep's clothing."

The irony that a pack of werewolves raised sheep was not lost on me here. I think I began piecing things together —but still didn't have enough to go on to make a sensible argument to the contrary.

Still, by the time Charity finished her tale, I had bells

ringing in my mind. Ding! Ding! Ding! Mags, you may have the answer.

"It's a witch."

All eyes turned to me.

"Believe what I saw in my vision when the werewolf ancestor of Francine's was skinned alive, coupled with what happened to the child. She came stuffed in a box and shipped here by some unknown, and the atrocity done to that poor possum—add it to what happened all those years ago with Johnny and Benji."

I contemplated the child who gazed solemnly at me, eyes wide and all thoughts of eating forgotten. Then I watched Johnny, who'd finished his meal and drifted across the ground back to the safety of his cabin. Finally, I connected the dots, albeit haphazardly, and came up with my solution.

"It's definitely a witch."

CHAPTER 8

"Explain, Mags," Antoine asked even as Charity gathered up the child and took her away from the conversation. But of course, little ears mustn't hear and all that, I guessed.

"It's a sense I got from the viewing. This person was powerful, wicked, and possessed some sort of magic to overpower a grown male werewolf in his wolf form. Francine said a witch gifted the Eskimo doll to her family who didn't know it had been cursed. They locked it away years after it began causing all manner of bad things to happen to the pack. What if the witch is the same as the one who skinned the wolf in my vision? Then she crafted the doll, giving it to his kin as some kind of sick offering?

"She? You think it's a female witch now?" asked Serena with interest.

"He... she. I'm not certain, but I'd almost swear on it after thinking things through and trying to visualize the hands holding the knife. I think we are dealing with a dark witch."

"Why is it always a dark witch? Can't we get something new and exciting to have to deal with?" grumbled Bella, stuffing a spoonful of potato salad in her mouth. Today she was sporting her full-on petulant teenager look: pigtails, roller skates, and short shorts. Earlier today, when we were doing the reading for Francine, Bella looked positively grown up in a pair of jeans and a blouse. Now? Now she morphed into a thirteen-year-old nightmare on wheels.

I think she did it so the little girl wouldn't feel so intimidated around all these adults.

Who knew she had a kind heart?

"What do you mean, 'why is it always a dark witch?' That's not true!" I scolded.

"Lately, that's what we've been dealing with. Your tribe is power-hungry, and there are way too many renegades running about."

"And what? Do we need to regulate the witch community now? Perhaps round them up and start burning them at the stake again?" I cried.

"Whoa! Calm down, Sparky! I was only making an observation. There are plenty of other rogue Breed out there—vampires and sirens are the worst offenders. Calm down!"

"Hey! We get a bad rap but most of us want to pursue our interests and have no compulsion to do anything nefarious!" exclaimed Tor with a frown.

"Yeah. Your interests usually involve sucking blood and having copious amounts of kinky vampire sex," scoffed Nathara.

Tor's scowl deepened, but he chose to refrain from arguing.

Seeing this descend to something all of us would regret later on if it got out of hand, I decided to take over the conversation—being the leader and all—and chose to set an example.

"And just how many witches have we had to deal with recently that has you two being such whiney babies about it?" I snarked at both Nathara and Bella.

Or not.

Bella screwed her face up and took a huge bite of chicken which she began to munch in a loud manner.

"Millicent and her doddering old sisters, Esther and Louise. The Old Higue on that same case. Victoria Leewood's coven and Silvara Stormsong's coven, not to mention crazy Vera and Nathara's role in that mess. Oh! And let's not forget my situation with the demented Olgav and the witch strix horror that she was. Then we met up with your crazy Sweet Briar family, demon-lovers, all of them, taking up with that insane Pandora. And Florin, the man behind Ellie's transformation." Bella took in a considerable amount of air and blew it out in a huff. "And don't get me started on that old bat!"

"Old bat?" I cried, puzzled because I didn't remember any bat in our recent cases.

"That Adriana Dolce. Do you know she put a numbing spell on Serena, Sydney, and me so Pandora could tie our hair together in braids? We came out of it only to stumble around shrieking from the pain, and it took us ten minutes to untangle that mess. The woman is a menace!"

"I lost a few locks of hair even," whispered Serena, wide-eyed.

"What about Barney? He isn't a witch. He's a Djinn. Last I checked, genies aren't kin to witch folk!" I argued.

"Yeah, but that Mary Beth, or Marabella, or whatever she called herself...she was a witch. Everything lately points to a plethora of rogue witches! And I've had it!"

I tried to remain calm, seeing as how Bella had a legitimate reason for being upset. After all, Olgav stole her baby sister away for centuries, and she didn't find her again until the crazed witch found us recently. So I could kind of see her point. Still, it wasn't all evil witches, and every other Breed was pure as snow.

"What about that teen in Greenville of Nathara's? She was a suicide that went poltergeist and..."

"Took drugs during a ritual in the woods. Dark witch," stated Nathara dryly.

Fine. There be bad witches afoot.

"Not all witches are bad! What about my cousin Lily? She's wonderful and..."

"Almost burned her town down, caused all manner of bedlam with her wayward spells, befriended a demon—not to mention a siren. A siren!"

"Last I checked, Serena and Sydney are succubae. You can't get more demonic than that! And what's wrong with sirens?" I screeched.

"And did I not mention Adriana?" Bella went on as if I hadn't asked a question or pointed out a flaw in her thinking. "Yeah... Lily's a carbon copy of that old bat. Just you wait. In another sixty years, it will be like having another Adriana Dolce running around turning people into weeds!" shouted Bella.

"Did she tell you that story as well?" asked Sydney. "Apparently, if people get on her bad side, Adriana turns them into weeds then hits them with Roundup. Then she sits back and watches them wither and die. Her husband is worse! He turned his enemy into a goat!"

I was blinking rapidly, trying to figure out how becoming a goat was worse than dying a slow death as a weed, all the while listening to the turncoats around me air their list of grievances. I felt my ire growing.

"Not all witches are evil. That would be like saying all

werewolves turn into savage beasts in the light of a full moon. Or all vampires enthrall their victims, using them to feed. Or all elementals manipulate matter to cause natural disasters and bring chaos, or all shifters use trickery and malice to spy and steal and..."

Johnny's voice trailed off as everyone turned his way. No one had seen him sneak back up to us, and he now stood behind me with his hand on my shoulder.

"Maggie is the only one of you lot who didn't doubt me upon hearing that wretched tale just now. The rest of you? So easy to judge when you've only heard one side of the story. There are far scarier things out there then a few rogue witches. And despite what Maggie has suggested, we are not dealing with a witch." Johnny paused and met the gaze of everyone present. "What we are dealing with is utter chaos."

Why did the air suddenly get downright frosty?

"What the heck could be worse than all of our Breed combined that you say such a thing?" Antoine asked Johnny.

Johnny took the seat near mine after I scooched over to make room for him.

Placing his elbows on the table then running his hands through his glossy black hair, he looked up and offered his explanation, and I for one, wanted to hide under my bed and cuddle Bob.

"What we're dealing with is a skin-stealer. A dark fae who feels endless hunger and stalks its victim, then peels the skin off their bodies to make a cloak, or braids them to chew on as a snack. They feed on their victims' eyeballs which is the only part of the body they crave, before finding another. Only it takes them months, and sometimes years, to add the new skin to their cloak or braid it for some other purpose, so by the time they are ready for their next target, they are deranged by their hunger and remain paralyzed until someone comes along close enough for them to latch on and repeat the process." Johnny shuddered and went on with his explanation. "Or they enthrall a young victim, making them bring them offerings—small animals, children, anything the youngling can manage to lure or maim enough times until the dark fae becomes strong again. Then they kill their thrall and continue down their dark path only to start it all over again."

"The fae are real?" squealed Dara, and I could see her fight not to cross herself. Dara waffles back and forth from her druidic paganism and a weird form of Catholicism with abandon.

"Aye, we've had a hoard of them in Scotland, and the British Isles, Ireland, even Iceland and Greenland have had reports of the beings staying in remote locations. Most of them keep to themselves, but when one of the fae turns dark, like a skin-stealer, they usually take care of it internally among their own. So how did this one slip through their grasp?" asked Tor.

"I don't know. Only I know the fae can take on human form, many of them disguised as older men or women...or in the paranormal world, they pass themselves off as a witch. I realized years ago what happened to Benji. He fell under the spell of a dark fae, and when I discovered his secret, he attacked me." Johnny finished his explanation then sighed, putting his head on my shoulder. "None in my pack would believe my tale. Werewolves don't believe in the fae—especially one who looked like a witch."

"And there you go! Witches again. Fairy witches!" cried Bella.

"Not fairies, lass," said Tor. "Fae. Entirely different

beings from your common pixies and fairy folk. I've heard it said they can even take on different personas, not unlike shifters."

"They are not like shifters...not at all," murmured Sven with a frown.

"Actually, they are." Tor refused to back down. "I've heard a dark fae can mimic a human so accurately that it would even fool one's own mother were she to come across it."

Well, that's going to keep me up tonight!

Who am I kidding? I wouldn't be sleeping much... I'd be pouring over Ellie's monster tomes and reading up on this dark fae. And here I'd spent all my recent recreational reading wasted on vampires!

CHAPTER 9

The next day I was tired, grumpy, and wandered bleary-eyed into my tiny kitchenette, hoping a cup—or three of coffee would wake me up. Bob followed me, seeking a refill of kibble and perhaps a teaspoon or two of his favorite canned food. Considering he ran off with a piece of my leftover chicken and wolfed it down before I could rescue it from his grasp, he had me giving him barely half a bowl filled with his breakfast.

Bob spent ten minutes staring at his bowl in disbelief at my hostility and pure evilness.

I didn't bat an eye when he mewed pitifully.

I walked over to the fairground next door, munching on an apple, contemplating the clear blue sky. It sure didn't seem like the end of the world was at hand, but I couldn't help feeling worried about this latest discovery and what we would do about it.

I had a long phone meeting with the Order, and my superiors promised to put the word out worldwide to see if any of the agents from other nations had any ideas or had dealt with the dark fae before. And in our case—a skin-stealer. We could use all the help we could get, so I was grateful for my bosses readily jumping into action.

It didn't hit me until later that morning when an older man turned up in my tent with some children's toys that had seen better days that I remembered we hadn't had time to search for the Ouija board. For prominently in his collection was another 1970s Milton Bradley game, and I became morose. I had to push that aside, however, and help him with his little problem.

"They're all possessed, darlin'. Every last one of them."

From what I could gather, he was a mixed bag of Breed. Part vampire, part mage like Tor with a bit of something else mixed in that I couldn't ascertain. Genie, perhaps? He did remind me a bit of good old Barney.

"I don't understand. How are all these board games possessed? I'm not sensing anything." I smiled to lessen the sting of my not believing him.

"Well, sweetheart, every time I go to play them with my grandbabies, the pieces begin to move all by themselves. Now, what kind of board game can do that, I ask you?"

I was still having difficulty concentrating because I had never considered a southern vampire before. And this man's drawl was so pronounced I had to keep from grinning after picturing him swooping down on a group of victims and saying, "I'm here to drink your blood, y'all."

"Have you tried using your magic on them?" I asked tentatively, knowing it might be considered impolite to divulge that I knew he had mage as well as vampiric blood.

"Oh, I'm useless there. My daddy didn't take kindly to my momma showing me any of that hocus-pocus, so I sorely lack my mage powers; more's the pity. So no, I just content myself in the knowledge I have my other skillset to fall back on." He said this while giving me a wink and a tip of his huge Stetson hat.

Nope. No way could I imagine this guy as a vampire.

"OK. Well, let me see what we have then, shall I?" Taking the top game, another old-time favorite called Trouble, into my hands, I peered around the edge then opened the box looking for some hex or glow or anything that would offer me an explanation of what I was dealing with for now.

Then I heard a telltale whining sound, ever so faint, but I instantly suspected I had the answer. So, picking up my cell phone, I quickly called Serena hoping she wasn't tied up with a client—and in Sydney and Serena's case, I meant that quite literally.

"What's up, boss lady?"

I cringed and sighed inwardly. Of course, I'd been getting plenty of that since outing myself as leader of this immoderate group of goofballs.

"Hey, can you come to my tent a minute? I have something I need to show you."

"Your wish is my command, oh, exalted one!"

This sort of crap needed to end quickly, or I'd be in a constant state of miffed and might never recover my charming and sunny disposition.

I can hear you laughing, so just stop now.

When Serena rushed into my tent, I was confident I had the right of it. "Here, examine these games. This gentleman thinks they are possessed, but I have a feeling we're dealing with another kind of mischief. What do you think?"

Serena came to my table, took a seat, and began going through each game carefully, opening the boxes and examining each piece until she paused, frowning.

"Gotcha! You can just come out of there, and I mean now!"

Motioning for me to have some vessel at the ready, I jumped up, grabbed an old Tupperware container, and waited for something to happen. It didn't take long for me to notice a minuscule blip peering up from under one of the Trouble pieces that toppled over suddenly. Once that happened, a large popping sound filled the room, and six or seven pixies materialized in front of us.

I didn't hesitate but froze them with my magic, then dropped them into my container, which I sealed shut.

"Well, you could knock me over with a feather! I didn't see that one coming! Them fairies are about as welcome as a porcupine at a nudist colony! So what do I owe you?"

I'll never forget this dude as long as I lived.

He certainly paid well despite my skepticism.

***

"Have you spoken with Derek or Charity?" I asked Antoine.

Despite the revelation that I was in charge of things, I was still in the habit of deferring to Antoine and didn't see myself changing things any time soon. That's why I suggested he seek out the pack leader and his mother and discuss what we'd discovered. I also hoped Antoine could reason with them and temper the pack's suspicion of Johnny, but only time would tell if they'd believe his story and accept him as their true leader. Or perhaps that was a bridge they'd never cross—or one Johnny wouldn't even desire them to, so much time and animosity had occurred among them.

I just hoped there would be some closure for his sake at least, and he'd reconcile with Charity.

"I have. Charity seems open to the idea of Johnny's innocence and the tale of the dark fae. Derek? Well...he's troubled and is holding judgment until we discover if we are dealing with this creature now or if it is some other kind of monster in their midst. Even The Order of Origin calling off their suspicions of the pack having a renegade hasn't brought him around yet."

Antoine looked as tired as I felt, and I wondered again about his constant state of fatigue. It had been this way ever since we stayed at my family compound in Mystic Valley, North Carolina. We weren't due back for rest and relaxation until the Christmas holidays, so I felt justified in my concern. If Antoine had something going on that needed looking into, I didn't want him putting it off until then.

"Antoine, is everything OK with you? I don't want to pry, but you seem down. No, more than that. You look utterly exhausted."

"I'll be fine, Mags. I'm just getting old, I guess."

I drew back and contemplated my friend, who didn't look a day over forty. "You can't be serious?"

"Perhaps I'm not. Maggie, I am well. Don't borrow any more trouble than is needed, OK?"

Fine. Be all secretive and stoic. I knew I'd get whatever was bothering Antoine out of him eventually.

We had just wrapped up another successful day, and my team was planning on grilling some steaks and having some thick-cut fries to go along with them. Perhaps even throwing in a salad to pretend we were health-conscious.

We were not.

Halloween was in two days, and we were feeling the stress of the entire celebration, what with a possible dark fae running loose and the mystery of the little girl still weighing us down.

"Hey, you two. Grab a dish and load up. Sven outdid himself with our meal," Bella called out to us. She was munching on a giant T-bone and had juice and grease all over her face. Seriously, anyone would swear she was fourteen and incorrigible. "Man, oh man, you can't beat a fresh steak in Texas. This baby was probably mooing yesterday."

Thanks for the visual, Bella.

We sat around a firepit when everyone had finished drinking coffee, and Sydney opened a bag of marshmallows that she mysteriously had stashed in her RV, and they began roasting them over the fire.

"So, what do we know?" asked Johnny, who suddenly looked a whole lot better, and I'm sure felt virtuous after everyone in our group apologized to him for their doubt—yours truly the exception since I'd never doubted him.

"It's what we don't know," stated Nathara. "One. Who delivered the trunk with that kid inside it to our tents and why specifically to Maggie? Is there a reason for that, or is it just a coincidence? Two, why a kid? What does she have to do with anything if all this is tied in some way? Three, is it tied somehow, or are there multiple levels of baloney going on? And just so you all know, baloney was not my first choice of words."

On that, I could wholeheartedly agree.

"Four, was the possum a warning, a taunt, or something else entirely?" asked Bella.

"Five, is it a coincidence again to have this Francine Adolpha show up who just happens to have this cursed Eskimo doll that brings the entire story front and center, or is she someone who needs a closer inspection? If what you said is true, Johnny, this Francine could be the dark fae taking on the form of another!" said Sydney darkly. "Perhaps we need to sniff her!"

"I could do that. Let's go find Francine and sniff her, sis," said Serena.

"Wait! Hang on. No one is sniffing anyone right now," I cried.

"Speak for yourself," chuckled Nathara throwing a glance in Sven's direction.

Oh! Ew.

I chose to ignore Nathara's comment and focused on keeping the two succubae from running off with Bella and accosting Francine, then start sniffing her. For some reason, the elemental and two minor demons did an awful lot of sniffing when examining someone, and I still couldn't get it out of them why they did so.

Needless to say, we didn't need an international incident where the werewolves around the world became insulted when three not of their kind stuck their noses where they didn't belong. I have no idea if werewolves sniffed each other, and a vision of dogs greeting one another suddenly had me unsettled. Great. I'd never look at Johnny in the same manner again as long as I lived.

"There's another thing to consider," stated Dara slowly as she sat with Madame Myna by her side. "Is this another coincidence that when we finally get a lead in Ellie's case, and it brings us here to Round Top, Texas, there just happens to be this incredulous occurrence that puts us off the trail for the time being? Or was this orchestrated so we'd be too busy trying to put out the fires here and not go out searching for the Ouija board in our spare time?"

Looking as shocked as I felt, Ellie hovered next to Dara and covered her mouth with one hand. Her eyes were large and round at the thought.

"But that would mean Florin Vulpe is in some way tied to all of this, and I can't imagine how…"

"Holy moly! I think I'm on to something here," cried Sven. "Give me a second."

Sven began to run something across this mind internally, then snapped his fingers in triumph.

"I'm correct. OK, listen up. Ellie gets attacked by a man who brought a tiny pewter wolf statue to your compound, right? So. The wolf again. In Romanian, Maggie and Ellie's mother's maiden name, Lupo, means wolf. Florin Vulpe's surname means fox. Francine's last name is Adolpho…that is German for a wolf. And this vision you had, Mags? The woman spoke Danish using the word 'ulv.' Wolf. Not to mention, here we are surrounded by werewolves."

Turning to gaze off into the direction of Charity's home across the field, Sven considered his following words and began to rub his chin. "And finally, that chest the little girl arrived in was heavily decorated with the image of foxes. How is that for one too many coincidences? And let's not forget Johnny's childhood story ties back to this dark fae who must be the same creature who slaughtered that werewolf, taking his pelt and making that Eskimo doll. After all, Francine is a distant relation of Johnny's!"

I did not like this. Not one bit.

CHAPTER 10

I turned in early, my mind awash with all I had heard this evening, and I knew I had to get to the bottom of this quickly, or we *did* need to cancel the Halloween festivities. We could not risk all the lives of the children that would be showing up to take part in the fun.

Ellie hadn't joined me in my RV, and I curled up in bed, holding Bob and thinking. My sister often disappeared around bedtime. She told me she never slept and that watching us eat while torturous, didn't mean she wanted to spend any more time away from us than necessary. Still, it couldn't be easy watching us dine while she spent her time in endless hunger...or at least constantly craving something of which she could not partake. To sit around here watching me sleep, as well would be ridiculous!

An hour went by, then another, and I realized slumber would not be coming for me this night, and I knew why.

Climbing out of bed, I padded over to the dresser and, opening the top drawer, pulled out the receipt that showed the last known location of that darned Ouija board.

Making a quick decision that I hoped I didn't live to

regret, I quickly dressed myself all in black from top to bottom, even pausing to slick back my hair and tie it up in a loose bun. This I covered in a black knit cap. Then, looking every bit the part of a cat burglar, I crept out of my RV and over to my Jeep depressing the brake pedal. Then I turned the key to the "on" position and put my vehicle in neutral. I began to push it away from camp—I may have used more than a little of my magic to move it along while sitting comfortably in the driver's seat, not doing any actual pushing from behind.

Once I cleared the drive and turned onto the main road, I turned to key over and started the engine, then drove off in the direction of Oldenburg...and hopefully the damned Ouija board. I opened the driver and passenger windows, enjoying the cool night air—not quite crisp yet. We were in Texas after all.

From my estimation and the GPS reading, Oldenburg was only ten minutes down the road. But it was not much of a town. The directions showed an address that wound up being in Fayetteville, Texas, another fifteen minutes further out in the country. Hitting the "Go" button on the navigation on my phone, I drove off into the night alone.

"And where are you going this fine evening, lass?"

"Sweet Jesus! Are you trying to kill me?" I just barely averted slamming on the brakes and swerving off the road.

"I don't think Jesus would be down with killing you, love. All that pacifism talk, and He being who He is and all," Tor said with a smile.

"You know what I mean, you depraved fangster. What are you even doing here? How did you know I'd left?! I was quiet!"

"I observed you as you listened to Dara speak of the Ouija board and all this as a distraction keeping us from it.

Your face transformed into an *aha* moment, and I knew you'd be nothing but trouble from that point forward, so I opted to sleep in the back seat here, knowing full and well you'd be sneaking out tonight."

"I don't sneak!"

"Yet you were doing just that."

"I told you, I was quiet. Being quiet out of consideration for those sleeping and sneaking away are two different things," I said through gritted teeth.

"Did you inform anyone you were heading out on your own to discover the Ouija board?"

I didn't answer right away and squirmed in my seat.

"You were sneaking," Tor said smugly.

"I didn't want to inconvenience anyone!"

"You keep telling yourself that, lass. But we both know what you were doing."

"You insufferable boor! Don't you dare tell me what I was or wasn't doing. You deceitful ass. You come here pretending to be something you're not and gain my trust, only then I find out you've been spying on me…"

"Margaret Fortune! I'm not here to spy on you."

"Magdalena."

"Come again?"

"It's Magdalena—my name. Everyone assumes I was named after my great aunt, and I was, but my mother liked Magdalena better and at the last minute put that on my birth certificate."

"Did she now!"

"She did."

"But people call you Margaret."

That's because my mother never told anyone what she did. I didn't find out myself until I went to get my driver's license and found out my legal name was Magdalena Isla

Fortune. Although I even introduce myself as Margaret Isla Fortune. And I don't know why I am telling you all this, but there you have it."

"It's beautiful. Magdalena Isla Fortune. As beautiful a name as is the woman."

"Oh, don't you start trying to soften me up. I can't believe how fraudulent you are!"

Tor sat back, disappearing from my sightline. I couldn't turn around to see what he was up to and tried to remain focused on the road.

Before I knew what had happened, Tor appeared in the front seat, and I screamed, hitting the brakes and causing him to fly into the dashboard, then threw the Jeep into park, and glowered at him even though he was rubbing his head and moaning. That time my actions gave me more satisfaction than having control.

I may even have done it on purpose.

"Jesus Christ, woman! Are you mad?" he growled.

"You have to ask? How did you do that?! One minute you are behind me, and the next, you are sitting beside me, acting all superior. You nasty vampire! You probably turned into a tiny bat and flew out the back and into the front without me the wiser. Then you'll explode into Dracula and think I'll swoon or something. And if you think for one minute, I'll...oomph!"

Tor crushed me into a hug and took my breath away when he landed one mind-blowing kiss on me.

It went on for quite some time, and I felt myself turning into molten lava. I was a puddle of goo. My senses were on overdrive, and all I wanted to do was crawl into Tor's lap and forget the world existed.

Pulling away from our embrace, Tor looked at me with

drunken, lazy eyes, all heat, lust, and smolder and said, "My God, but you're incredible when you're angry."

I'm doomed.

∼

"That's a chicken coop."

"That is not a chicken coop; it looks like a... what do you call the thing they store sheep in?"

"I didn't know one stored sheep."

"You know what I mean!" I grumbled.

"I'm not quite sure that I do, love."

I sighed. Loudly. "You know...a pen, a coop...a..."

"Sheepfold?"

"Sheepfold! That is a sheepfold."

"It looks like a chicken coop, but maybe you do things differently here in the States."

Tor's words gave me pause, and I suddenly got the impression he wished he'd not uttered those words to me just now.

"I thought you were from North Carolina?" I asked.

"I've been there. My sister lives there...and my mother."

"But you're from Scotland. I see. Is there anything else you haven't told me? No. Forget I asked. You'll just lie."

"Maggie."

"No, it's OK. I should have known. I mean, you have a slight accent and all. Why didn't I question it? Probably because I knew you were too good to be true and..."

"Maggie."

"Really, I'm fine. It would never have worked out, what with you being an ancient immortal and me a witch. I'm not even a dark witch. Mostly I'm a psychic and tamper any witch abilities I have. I probably bore you so..."

"For Heaven's sake, woman! Would you shut it and look over there by the chicken coop?"

"Sheepfold. Why am I... oh! What is that?" I strained my neck to get a better view from our cramped position scrunched down behind the wooden fence.

"I believe that is a llama."

"But I thought this was supposed to be a sheep farm?"

"Maggie, let's worry about that later and get a move on."

"But we need to go check the place out. Why would you want to leave when we just got here?"

"Lass, it might be a sheep farm, but farmers often keep llama to guard them. Now...run!"

I turned back toward the meadow only to have a scream lodge in my throat. A very angry-looking llama was tearing across the field at us, and I for one, didn't want to find out what a llama did on the defensive...or was that offensive? Either way, I wanted no part of it, so I ran as fast as I could back to the safety of my Jeep.

"Maggie, lass. Why did you want to cross the field and see the sheep, anyway?" Tor asked when we accessed the situation from my front seat and found the llama standing guard at the fence line.

"I didn't want to see the sheep. I thought if we sneaked around the outbuildings, we'd have a better vantage point to see the best way into the house. After all, if someone here purchased the Ouija board, it would be in the house—not the sheep pen."

"Indeed."

"And as it's the middle of the night, I figured we'd have to slip in unannounced and look around so..."

"In the dark."

"Well, yes. In the dark, but I hadn't quite figured out that part yet."

"Nor what you'd do if you got caught, I gather."

I frowned at his tone. "I could always use a spell."

"And what pray tell would you do if they turned out to be ancients?"

"Ancient what?"

Tor looked to the heavens as if seeking advice on what to do with me.

"Ancient anything, lass! Vampires, elementals, shifters...you name it. Your magic wouldn't stand a chance up against something that antediluvian."

"Anti-de-whosy-what?"

"Old. That old."

He had a point. I guess I just hoped they'd be a lovely older couple, farmers who just happened to want the Ouija board circa 1890 and didn't practice witchcraft—or worse.

"I guess I didn't think this through."

"Do me a favor."

"What?" I was feeling rather inept and embarrassed that I hadn't strategized about what I'd do once I got here.

"Stay here. Keep the car running, and don't follow me."

"Follow you where?"

"I'm going in."

And in a flash, Tor was in the front seat one minute and gone the next. I didn't even see him disapparate or whatever freaky Harry Potter disappearing act he'd just pulled off. Vampires are decidedly slippery beings.

CHAPTER 11

"Oh, my goodness! Oh, my goodness! You got it. I can't believe you found it!"

We were back in my RV, and I was staring at the Ouija board, not truly believing it was sitting on my dinette table. I stood beside it and grinned at Tor, who stood near the entrance as if trying to decide whether or not he was staying or leaving. He was smiling but seemed distracted. I, however, was buzzing with energy.

"We need to open it, Tor."

"Yes, we do, but not now, lass."

"But we have it. It might lead us to a cure for Ellie. So, we have to open it."

"Maggie. It's three-thirty in the morning, and Dara has the key. I don't think she'd appreciate being awakened for something that can wait until later today.

But I wanted to get my hands on that map. I began to worry my bottom lip then peered up at Tor.

"You're still bleeding, and I don't look much better. I can't believe you went into that tiny closet then fell into the basement through the hole in the floor!"

"I can't believe you disobeyed me and followed me into the house and closet, and you also fell into the hole in the floor and down to the basement. Landing on top of me, I might add."

"That dog was certainly huge."

"Cane Corso. It's an Italian breed used for protection."

"Yes, well...he did his job a little too well. I'm sorry he bit you. I didn't know if vampires could bleed or what, and I tried to help when he clamped down on you."

"As you can see, we definitely bleed. But it's already healing. I will be fine by morning. You, on the other hand, need some tending to." Tor took a step in my direction.

"I got stuck in those brambles. I'm not sure what they were. It was too dark. I ran when the farmer and his wife called out to the dog. They frightened me; both had their false teeth out, and the man had a shotgun."

"Blackberries and probably covered in chiggers are yeh now."

"I should take a shower." I moved a smidge in the direction of the bathroom and closer to Tor. "I'm just glad you charmed those two, and now they believe we were Jehovah's Witness missionaries and took the Ouija board for their own good."

"Aye. Take your shower, lass. It will probably make you sleepy."

"Oh, no! I don't think I will be able to sleep a wink. I'm too hyped up. Plus, my neck aches from how I landed when I jumped out the upper bedroom window."

"I still don't know why you ran up the stairs when all we had to do was to run out the back door. You should let me rub that." Tor made to move closer and got halfway over to me but stopped when I raised my hands.

"I'm fine. Really. I'm just glad the farmer and his wife

are hard of hearing and had their hearing aids out and charging. I don't know what they'll think when they find the mess we left; maybe they'll blame it on their dog. Who keeps something so fierce wandering around the house like that?"

"Deaf farmers that want to sleep in peace."

I guess.

"Well, maybe they'll assume we rummaged around in the basement, found the Ouija board and decided to save their souls. I better let you go so I can take that shower. Thank you for saving me from that snarling brute. I'm sorry he bit your, um, posterior."

"I'm sure I'll live."

"Ha. Live. Yeah, um...so, I guess I will see you tomorrow then." I took another step toward Tor, and we were now an arm's length apart. "Today rather. Go get some sleep or something."

"I rarely sleep." Tor closed the distance, so he was now in my personal space.

I swallowed and looked up into his smoldering eyes.

"Well, I will be awake right along with you. I'm too keyed up to sleep. Plus, it will take me an hour to get the brambles out of this hair of mine."

Tor looked at my hair, then reached out and tried to run his hand through it. It got stuck, which wasn't surprising.

"I could help you with that."

"With what?"

"Untangling your hair."

I swallowed again, but my mouth went suddenly dry. "Oh, I usually do that in the shower."

"Yes."

I opened my mouth to say something witty, but Tor reached out and pulled me into a passionate kiss, and I went willingly into his arms. Even though I was still mad at him for...what was I angry at him for again?

"Let me wash your hair, Magdalena."

"Only if you let me tend to your wounds."

"Even the one on my bum?" He pulled back and smiled at me with mirth dancing in his wicked eyes. They instantly sobered at my following words.

"Yes. I will make all your hurt go away."

Tor crushed me to him once more, our mouths meeting and our hands exploring, and I couldn't help but notice his fangs had protruded slightly. It sent a thrill down to my toes.

I didn't notice Ellie swish into the room, nor did I hear her gasp and spin around, heading back out through the wall to wherever it was she went at night. I didn't see Bob skid into the kitchenette hoping for a late-night snack only to hiss and arch when Tor lifted me into his arms and carried me to the back of the RV. I also didn't notice that my anger with Tor had slipped into something akin to a frenzied passion that only one thing would sate.

I suppose I could wait until sometime later that day to see what we'd find inside the Ouija board. But right now, a hot vampire was going to wash my hair...and other things.

CHAPTER 12

We never did get to bed. Well, we got to bed, but we didn't sleep.

Anyway...around nine or so, we wound up near our picnic area, finding everyone but Ellie, Johnny, and Dara present.

Trying to act nonchalant, like I'd not just had the most incredible night of my life, I wandered over to the makeshift outdoor kitchen and poured myself a coffee. I didn't bother asking Tor if he wanted any as he was already sitting next to Sven and Antoine, looking at the schematic they'd drawn up for tomorrow's Halloween party. So I went to sit beside Serena, grabbing an orange cranberry muffin along the way.

I was trying not to think of my concerns, all the points I had brought up about why getting involved with a vampire would be a bad idea. I also kept thinking about what Tor explained was a clandestine mission he was on and that it did not involve evaluating my performance as head of the US division of our secret group. Secret missions, secret groups...I responded I didn't much like secrets, at least not between lovers, to which he replied, "I agree, but I still can't let you get involved with what mine is."

I had to respect that because I'd say the same thing if I were in his position.

Tor also assured me neither of us outranked the other as far as the Order was concerned. I informed him I didn't like being under anyone, and he responded with a cheeky, "That's perfectly fine since I like you on top." Ahem. *Yeah.* Just recalling that had me blushing again.

"What's up with you?" asked Nathara, looking at me curiously.

"What? I didn't say a thing. I'm having coffee. What's up with you?"

Sydney tilted her head then looked at her sister. Serena turned to regard me a moment, then slapped her hand over her mouth. Bella raised her head from her plate. She'd been consuming an omelet and had a mouthful so that she couldn't speak. But her eyes got wide, and she made nonsensical sounds while trying to swallow in a hurry. I was getting nervous and looked from one friend to the other warily, then shrugged and began to eat my muffin.

"Oh my God."

I paused with the muffin halfway to my mouth.

"What?" I asked, irritation clouding my voice.

"You guys did it! You did the nasty with Tor, and don't even try to deny it!" cried Serena.

"Oh, she did it. She's glowing!" said Nathara. Sydney nodded in agreement.

"You had hot kinky vampire sex, and you're alive to talk about it?" asked Bella, her voice rising in crescendo.

All eyes turned toward me, and a silence fell over our party. I flicked my eyes over to Tor, who gazed at me. A barely imperceptible twitch to his lips had me acknowledge he was in a teasing mood. He stood and came to where I was sitting, still holding the muffin halfway to my open mouth.

"Here, love. Let me help you with that." Tor plucked the muffin out of my hand, straddled the bench, then broke off a piece and gently fed it to me before wiping the corner of my mouth with a napkin.

"Sweet Jesus," whispered Bella.

Tor waited until I finished chewing, then fed me another, and then another bite until my muffin was gone. Then he leaned forward and brushed his lips gently to mine, his fangs extended ever so slightly, before getting up and strolling back to where Antoine and Sven were sitting, mouths agape.

"Find me some of that, sister. That's what I need in my life," murmured Sydney.

"You and me both, Syd. You and me both."

After our public display of wanton lust, I became rather shy and wanted to hide under my covers. When I considered what I'd just been doing *on* said covers, I blushed from ear to ear. This time there was no doubt that I needed a cold shower. Instead, I cleared my throat and asked a question.

"Has anyone seen Dara today?" I managed to squeak out, sounding like a mouse.

"She's still in her...or rather, Antoine's RV. It seems like you're not the only one getting busy around here," smirked Nathara.

"Children. Please. What do you need with Dara, Mags? Or can I help?" asked Antoine.

"Oh, I need that key which opens the Ouija board, you see. Tor found it last night."

"And Maggie helped," said Tor with a wide grin.

"I bet," said Nathara. "I just bet."

Our enthusiasm for finding the Ouija board had tempered when the arrival of several local werewolf packs caused an all-hands-on-deck moment. Charity was running about setting sites up for folks and passing out information about tomorrow's festivities—specifically, no costumed masks for adults and little makeup to conceal. Only the children could be decked out all the way. Most adults understood when hearing about our troubles.

A few grumbled, but other than that, we had one worry ticked off our list.

We broke apart for a while, then duty called. Today was our last day doing appraisals and buying and selling antiques. Tor had a stack of old books he was eager to go through, and a collector from Round Top would be there to do some kind of exchange or purchase.

Sven was busy appraising military items from the revolutionary and civil wars, with Serena and Sydney looking on; they were weapons experts.

Bella had her hands full with a pack of teenagers who brought her arcane objects, or so they said, to be appraised and deemed free of anything "spooky." Considering these were humans teens and most of the items were Harry Potter memorabilia and Twilight novels, I think we were safe in concluding they'd be free from the paranormal—although you never knew!

Thankfully, I had an uneventful day but made a tidy profit. Always a plus in my book.

Later that evening, we dined on takeout from a local barbecue joint, and I was in hog heaven! Sipping on sweet lemonade, I was half-listening to our final meeting before tomorrow's Halloween event but focused when Serena took the floor.

"About that alarm," she said. "We have some issues to talk about."

Serena pointed out we hadn't reset our alarm, and Bella suggested waiting just before the Halloween activities started tomorrow. "This way, we can weave the web of magic, and as the families arrive and cross, it will only sound if and when something purely evil follows them...and we can dial it down low, more of an annoyance instead of loud bells and whistles."

We agreed, and that was the next thing ticked off the list.

I was about to discuss this evening's activities and get the stats on our sales for the day when a piercing scream echoed around camp.

"What the heck?"

Every member of my team rose to their feet and took off in the direction of the scream. It didn't take us long to find the werewolf child standing between the tent I shared with Bella and the one Tor and Johnny worked out of, which was secured.

The child stood close to the female police officer from the other day, who was lying on the ground very much dead.

~

"This is a disaster!" Charity Baldoni was wringing her hands and trying to remain calm despite stating the obvious. The last thing any of us wanted was the human world being pulled into our world by murder. And this was definitely murder.

The officer was lying on her back and looked like some kind of animal mauled her to death—she was missing skin, and her neck was a hideous mess. Considering werewolves surrounded us, it didn't look good for the pack. Ellie was hovering around the cops that arrived with Lieutenant Foster, who seemed puzzled when meeting with us. Understandable, since we'd wiped his memory of the child, but he still remembered my people.

"I don't understand why Officer Jackson was even here. Did any of you call her?"

"No. We had no reason to. We'd just ended our appraisals for the day and were discussing tomorrow's Halloween party when one of the workers discovered her lying here," I explained.

We didn't mention the child had discovered the body, not wanting to push it with the lieutenant's memory...or lack thereof.

"Does anyone around here have guard dogs or know of a pack running wild? I'm no expert, but I think this is a dog attack...or wolf."

"There aren't any wolves in Texas, right?" Johnny asked, looking far more nervous than he should. Especially in front of the lieutenant.

"Of course not. Not unless they're in a zoo. I'll have to make some calls and wait for the medical examiner to call it. In the meantime, this area is off-limits, and I need to conduct some interviews."

Thankfully, our gear was packed up and had been moved to the semi-trucks. All that was left was the tents. But the police tape being so close to where we were having a Halloween party might not go over well. Then again, most folks coming were werewolves and witches, and they don't scare easily. In a ghoulish way, it might even enhance the spooky ambiance.

We moved off to the periphery of the police investigation, watching as Ellie kept close enough to overhear the goings-on. No one wanted to speak much, and I briefly wondered if this would have my father showing up and pulling his weight. We weren't on the best of terms right now. Dad was currently living with three women—one of whom was a witch from a coven that had given us a bit of trouble, so understandably, I was not thrilled about the situation—let alone the other two women all sharing his bed at the same time.

I wasn't a prude—much—but I didn't approve of my dad's behavior or the careless way he treated the women in his life, and that included his two daughters. Ellie wasn't happy either, and the brief reconciliation they'd shared when Caliente Saunders, our vampire friend, had enabled it so everyone paranormal could see and hear my sister, the relationship between Dad and Ellie returned to being strained.

In any case, the last thing I wanted was for my father to show up and cause a scene.

"Maggie, did you notice that group of werewolves that arrived today?" Antoine pointed with his chin, and I stared at the pack he'd indicated.

"I hadn't paid them much attention. What's up?"

"They keep scenting the air, and it's drawing attention from the human element. The leader keeps circling our camp and then heads over toward Johnny's house and his mother's place beyond, then circles back. They are making me nervous—and not much makes me nervous, Mags."

"Do you think they will flip? I mean, nothing is threatening them exactly. We don't know who or what did this, and I... whoa. Do you think it's one of the new packs that arrived?"

"Perhaps. We need to put patrols out and especially keep to the plan tomorrow."

Indeed. We were expecting close to sixty children and their families. I didn't want to think of what could go wrong if things got out of hand, especially with some kind of nefarious creature running loose.

"We've got this, Antoine. Tonight, we can run teams out and see if we can pick up a trail, and tomorrow it will be an all-hands-on-deck effort. Let's hope the visiting packs give us the courtesy of behaving and obeying the rules and not getting it into their heads that we need their help."

"They're a suspicious bunch on a good day. Right now? They look like they want to start a fight," said Antoine.

"I think we have more to worry about than antsy werewolves," replied Tor. "We more than likely have a renegade among them, and I have a feeling they won't be content with the murder of that policewoman. Whoever is doing this intends to strike again."

We all knew he spoke the truth.

"Why do you think the officer was attacked here so close to us?" asked Ellie, who drifted over.

"I think it was a warning. Or maybe whoever is doing this is testing us to see what we'll do?" I replied.

"Did you notice her cell phone was smashed and broke open? It looks like whoever did this might have taken her by surprise or caught her taking photos. Maybe even overheard her talking on the phone. Perhaps she saw something—like our culprit. That's the only thing that makes any kind of sense," said Antoine.

"Do you think the child saw something?" asked

Nathara, glancing toward the police to make sure they weren't in earshot.

"It won't do us any good to ask—she refuses to speak," I grumbled.

"Right now, we need to stay alert. I don't think any of us want something like this to happen again." Antoine looked at all of us to make sure we understood just how dangerous a situation this turned into.

I certainly hoped nothing else would occur before or during the Halloween event.

I was not too fond of our odds.

CHAPTER 13

Halloween dawned with a gloomy overcast of fog and mist. I finished my coffee and left Tor and the gang to tackle the few problems regarding the party tonight. Tor spent the night on guard duty and informed me he'd go off and take a nap away from all the hullaballoo and would see me later in the day. Of course, vampires don't need much sleep, but mine was exhausted.

Wait. When did Tor become mine again?

When I decided to be mature and not hold a grudge, and his wandering hands became a distraction, not to mention his kissing abilities and other things.

Ahem.

I met up with Charity first thing and she informed me she hoped to get information out of the child, yet she steadfastly refused to speak. A dead end as far as we were all concerned. Hopefully the trauma of finding the dead policewoman wouldn't scar her even more. Now Charity's concerns turned to the weather.

The fog was thick and swirling—perfect for the mood of the day, but it couldn't have come at a worse time. The pack and coven leaders expressed concerns for their children, and Charity had spent a good two hours assuring everyone that she had things well in hand.

She did not.

Especially since, as far as the werewolves were concerned, they wanted no part of the little girl who'd shown up under mysterious circumstances.

Charity tried to introduce her to all the leaders and their families, but they immediately shunned the child, and some went so far as to demand she not be present at tonight's activities. Unbeknownst to the rest of us, werewolves were a highly suspicious lot. With no one around to lay claim to her, a solitary child didn't bring out maternal or paternal feelings—quite the opposite. It was as if they blamed the little girl for being rejected, abducted, or whatever predicament she was in, and they didn't want her negativity around their children.

None of us could comprehend their attitude, but then again, none of us were werewolves except for Johnny.

I spent the rest of the morning dealing with the uneasy sense that something was heading our way. Something evil. I spent last night reading anything I could find on dark fae, and it wasn't much. The fae are elusive, remain far from the world of men—and the various Breed. They keep to themselves in remote locations and usually are harmless. While the light fae are generally neutral—no one would ever say they were completely good—it was the dark fae who were the ones to cause mischief and mayhem.

And there were over three hundred varieties of the dark fae!

The dizzying number of characteristics, diversity, and type of these creatures left me reeling. Who knew? I mean, seriously. I always thought of them as fairy tales, but what kind of idiot did that make me? On some level, the paranormal world knows of the fae. But when no one reported seeing them for centuries, I guess we put them in a box in our minds and tucked them away in an attic somewhere to deal with another day.

That day was here if Johnny was accurate in his estimation.

Before I knew it, the time had arrived to don my Halloween outfit and get in a festive mood. I briefly wondered if the little girl would take part or if she'd shy away from all the other children who were now running amok like packs of rogue banshees.

I looked over to where the girl was quietly playing by herself and tried to feel some sympathy for her, but just then, she raised her head and frowned at me. Then, when I smiled and waved, she bared her teeth and growled.

I hate kids.

Ungrateful little beast! Bella and I went out of our way to find her! I kept wondering why she was delivered here. To my tent specifically.

"Nathara."

I called to the dark witch who was walking by with what looked like Halloween decorations. "Can I ask you something?"

"I don't give out free kinky sex advice."

"So funny...not. No, it's about that child. She hasn't spoken. She only growls at me when I try to engage her. Do you think something happened to traumatize her? Obviously, getting tossed in a chest and delivered to us had to be scary. But if what Johnny said is true, and we're dealing with a skin-stealing dark fae? Could it have damaged her in some way?"

"Perhaps. I mean, the girl is acting all normal right now,

but you never know. Do you want me to try and speak with her?"

"No. You have enough to do with the decorations, but in a bit, when we start handing out goodies, I think someone should keep an eye on her. Maybe all of us need to take turns."

"You think something is going to happen tonight." It was a statement, not a question.

"Yes."

Nathara nodded and continued on her way, and I decided to check on Bob and top off his food and water bowls. Plus, I was tired and hoped to close my eyes for ten minutes before putting on my witchy makeup.

"Where's my big boy? Hmmm? Where's my sweet boy?" I crooned when I walked into my RV.

Instead of Bob coming to run and greet me, I felt arms go around my waist, and I fell back into somebody's chest. Not hesitating for an instant, I made myself a dead weight by bending my knees and elbowing the person in the crotch. Then I tucked, rolled, and recovered, standing to my full height again.

"Oh, crud. I'm so sorry."

"For feck's sake, woman! I might be a vampire, but that still hurts."

"What are you doing hiding in my home? What was I supposed to do? Wait and see if you were a baddie or not first?"

"Did you not hear me tell you I'd see you later and that I'd find a nice quiet place to nap...then mentioned your sofa with Bob on my lap for company?"

"Vaguely? I'm sorry. I've been running around all morning and skipped lunch, and now it's time for this thing today. I am worried about dark fae and evil asshats and... and... I really hate kids!"

"Do you now? No plans for little witches... or?"

Or? Did he seriously ask me something important here, or was that teasing? I gulped and tried to smile, but I think I came across as a bit demented. His lips twitched again.

"Um. I have Bob."

"Ah, yes. Bob. He makes a fine napping companion."

"It's his favorite pastime."

I suddenly became shy but wanted nothing more than to kiss this vampire silly. Something must have registered in mine, for his eyes went molten, and he took a step in my direction. Then the screaming started.

"Bob! What is wrong with you?"

My tubby tuxedo cat was just at peace, gazing out the window and not paying us any mind when he exploded in a cacophony of ire and fury. Bob arched his back, and his fur was sticking straight up; tail triple its usual size!

"Merooow!"

"I don't see anything out there that he... oh! It's that little girl. She must have followed me over. Why is Bob acting up?"

"Is it the girl or that group of werewolves stalking her?" stated Tor as he came to stand behind me.

Would you look at that? There was a group of werewolves stalking the child! Well, maybe not stalking, but there were a group of two men and three women staring at her like she needed a good thrashing, or they intended to make a tasty snack out of her within the next five minutes.

Not good.

Sighing because now I wouldn't get that kiss in, I made a move to head out and confront the group when Tor spun me around, delaying me. "Not before we finish what we started, lass."

The kiss he gave me was toe-curling, firework-inducing, panty-dropping amazing, but alas, I had priorities being head of my organization and all.

Darn it.

"Hold that thought," I murmured a bit breathlessly as I marched out of my RV and over to the pack, switching from light-headed to intensely pissed off. I mean, a girl likes her private time, and these yokels were keeping me from my vampire-kissing endeavors—not to mention alone time with Tor to hash out just where the heck we were going with this...um...whatever it was we were doing.

"Can I help you?" I asked a bit heatedly.

"You can get out of the way so we can capture that child. She is an abomination!" said one of the women.

"Look, lady. I don't particularly like kids myself, but don't you think that's a bit much?"

"Much? Have you smelled her? She is no ordinary werewolf offspring. She has the scent of something feral and mentally unstable!" cried one of the men.

Perhaps that is why her pack abandoned her...if they did. Or it could be the trauma of whatever happened to her to be captured, put in a box, and shipped to us.

"She's been through a lot. You need to show some compassion!" I cried.

When all five adults moved in my direction with a level of hostility I wasn't expecting, I quickly removed my gloves, allowing my magic to coil up and spark—so my fingertips were glowing. Unfortunately, this didn't seem to impress the werewolves the way I'd hoped, and I squared my shoulders and faced them off, despite being outnumbered.

It wasn't until I sensed Tor behind me that the five

pulled up short and gave us a wary look. One witch against five werewolves had a slight chance to come out on top. Five werewolves against one vampire? Not so much. Although they departed, the two of us standing our ground was enough to garner a sneer of disdain and a show of teeth. I was left shaking and disturbed. What was wrong with these people?!

"Thanks for having my back," I said to Tor with a bemused smile in his direction. He was still on alert and looked too good for words.

"Always, lass. But you could have taken them. I've seen you fight."

Aw...shucks.

"Perhaps. But it was nice knowing you'd clean up the bodies afterward."

"Indeed. We'd toast with a nice blood-red wine after depositing them in a mass grave."

"I could get down with that."

And they say vampires aren't romantic. This man is pushing all the right buttons with his after-confrontation banter. A girl could lose herself in all that talk!

"I still am holding you to a full explanation of why you deceived me and what you are once you have the all clear to tell me, buster."

"You'll be the first one I inform."

I watched the shadows slowly creep closer and knew it was high time I don my costume and join the festivities already in high gear. But in reality, all I wanted to do was curl up with this man and while away the hours with some serious kanoodling and nonsensical talk.

"See you in a bit? What are you wearing, anyway?" I asked.

"A turtleneck and slacks. Was I supposed to be wearing something in particular?" Tor asked.

"I was kind of hoping you'd show up in a kilt."

"No costumes for adults, remember?"

"It's technically not a costume…but yeah."

Darn this mysterious, skin-stealing party pooper!

"Well, I'm one of the few allowed to dress up. So, I'm just doing my face a bit more, well, witchy, and will be all in black. Such the stereotype, but the kiddos will appreciate it while I'm handing out candy with Nathara. How I got stuck with that job, I will never know!"

"I can't wait to see you."

"Until later," I said, watching as Tor disappeared into the murky evening. The fog was now as thick as I'd ever seen it, and I twirled around happily, preparing to head back into my RV.

"He likes you."

I stopped short. Looking around to see who'd addressed me, I was shocked when realizing the little girl, forgotten in all the excitement, had spoken.

"Um…yes. Tor does, doesn't he? Are you OK?"

"I'm fine. Thank you for saving me from the others. They don't understand."

"Understand what, honey? Can you tell me your name?" I squatted down to be on her level, only slightly unnerved that a hitherto completely silent child was now, suddenly, loquacious.

"That I'm different for a reason. My name is Jessica."

OK, then.

"Different from what, Jessica?"

"Different from everyone…because I'm not normal."

Well. That was unexpected.

"And who told you that, sweetie? The person who put

you in the chest and sent you to us?" I was hoping the question would open the floodgates that seemed to have cracked a bit wider.

"No one sent me to you, silly. I came because it was ordained I be here at this time."

Whoa. This conversation went from mildly interesting to surreal. My alarm bells began to go off, and I gave the little girl my utmost focus. "What do you mean by that?"

"I've been looking for you. But now I need another...friend."

Friend? Looking?

"Me? You've been..."

"Well, not you, specifically. But..."

"Maggie! There you are. I need some help with the candy distribution, and you aren't even in makeup yet! Seriously! You bark out the orders but never follow through with them when it comes to you!" Nathara grumped.

"I was having a conversation with the little girl. She began talking, told me her name is Jessica and..."

"What little girl? You were standing here talking to thin air!"

I was what?

Moving my head from side to side, I searched for the child, but she wasn't there. I didn't see her scamper off, nor did I sense movement. How could that be? I might be tired, but I wasn't that tired.

"The girl in the box! She was right here!"

"Well, she isn't now! Hurry up, please! Get your stuff on and meet me over near Johnny's cabin. He decorated it to look like a creep show, and it's flooded with children hungry for candy and taking no prisoners!"

With that statement, Nathara swept off into the fog, leaving me scratching my head. I knew I needed to find the child, but duty called, and I couldn't abandon Nathara to little ghouls, goblins, and witches. She didn't like the little monsters any more than I did. And if there is one thing I know about children, they can sense those who intend to avoid them and go on the offensive.

Nathara and I might be frenemies, but I wouldn't abandon one of my people to such horror.

Time for some Halloween fun!

Why did I have a feeling it would be anything but?

CHAPTER 14

I spent the next three hours in hell.

You judge.

However, dealing with human children at a Halloween event is nothing compared to doing the same with a passel of paranormal hoodlums, all looking for candy and excitement. These kids *are* what goes bump in the night, so being a witch for the evening and handing out treats wasn't good enough for the little darlings. They wanted tricks as well.

At first, I didn't comprehend until one particularly smug ghost, not sure what Breed this kid was, but dressed up in a tiny white sheet with eyes cut out left me no delusions as to what they were pretending to be—asked me to give them a show—a magic show.

So, for the last hour, I'd been doing elemental witch magic nonstop, and I was feeling somewhat peckish.

Tor came by before heading off to the field to supervise the pumpkin chucking competition. He'd stopped cold in his tracks and wolf-whistled when he saw my long-sleeved spidery lace top, tight leggings, and over-the-top makeup that transformed me into an enchanting sorceress—at least in his estimation. I felt like a dork!

Everyone on my team was participating and had toned-down costumes on while entertaining the masses—except for Tor, who was indeed wearing a simple turtleneck.

Charity appeared beleaguered but content that her event was going off without a hitch. Even Johnny got into the action, transforming into his wolf—easily three times larger than an average one, giving the younger children rides on his strong back while parading around like something out of a nightmare. The kiddos squealed in delight. Seriously, nothing could phase these little beasts!

"Who's the chick?" Nathara asked, jutting her chin in the direction of Johnny's cabin.

A woman bedecked in what could only be described as a dark Little Bo Peep costume stood in the yard. She was all in black in Bo Peep style carrying a shepherd's hook but sporting a mask that you'd typically see during Mardi Gras or carnival—fancy and feathered.

"I don't know. No adult is supposed to be in disguise! I'd better..."

Just then, a commotion reached our ears coming from the main field. A hoard of werewolves came running in our direction, the five from earlier leading the pack.

Charity came rushing over to confront them as they reached us, and I felt my magic click on, despite being weary and feeling depleted from entertaining the children. It also occurred to me that our silent alarm had been sounding on and off for the last ten minutes. A pity we had all become so used to it, no one really paid it much attention. Our mistake.

"Where is the child? We chased her in this direction.

Someone needs to examine her!" cried the woman who'd spoken to me earlier.

"Stop this, Beverly. I told you she is frightened and hurting. Why must you insist on this drama?" cried Charity.

"Your pack has a history of not following through when bad things transpire. This child is not normal, and instead of doing what you know is right, you shelter her." So stated a man who I'd not seen previously. He was a big, hairy brute and looked every bit the werewolf.

Johnny abandoned the children and came padding over, growling and bristling at the visiting pack. Charity held her hand out to forestall his advance and prevent him from doing something he might regret.

Before anyone could do or say anything else, we heard a child scream out and watched in horror as the Little Bo Peep woman snatched her up and flashed away toward the tree line and creek.

The entirety of those in attendance remained shocked and paralyzed for a split second, and it wasn't until Nathara and I booked it in the direction she'd run that everyone came to life.

Shouting to Johnny over my shoulder as I ran to catch up to Nathara, I ordered him to transform and fetch Antoine and the rest of the team. Whether or not he heard me or comprehended what I was saying was another matter, but I didn't have time to worry about it now. First, I had to capture that demented Bo Peep!

Slightly winded but determined to find the abductor, I caught up to Nathara, who was searching for an indication of which way the woman had disappeared once she'd reached the creek.

I noted Nathara wasn't breathing heavily in the slightest and felt mildly irritated.

"Anything?"

"Ugh. No, and we'd better decide which way to head because here comes the brigade!"

Turning to behold three packs of werewolves running at us full tilt, I groaned inwardly and wished I'd never agreed to help with a Halloween party in werewolf territory.

"There! Listen!" I didn't have to listen; I'd already heard a shrieking child, and my blood ran cold. It came from our north, and Nathara and I wasted no time, wading across the creek and tearing off in the direction of that horrible sound—but not before I tossed out a magical blockade of sorts.

It wouldn't stop the werewolves—not entirely—but it would slow them down when they ran smack into my potent spell.

"Good thinking!" called Nathara, who was ahead slightly. I'd have to lay off my morning heavily-sweetened coffee and Danish if I hoped to be as limber and quick as the dark witch. She was gaining ground even as I struggled to keep up.

We ran to the following field and through groves of trees, then crossed another area, all the while catching glimpses of the costumed woman and screaming child. Feeling a distinct twitching pain in my side, I didn't know how much longer I could keep it up, but that's when we burst into another clearing and found Jessica.

What was she doing here?

"Jessica! Did you see a woman run by with a little girl just now?"

Laughing, Jessica cocked her head at us, shaking it back and forth. "No, no, no. You have it all wrong, Maggie Sweet."

"Did you ever tell her your name?" whispered Nathara in a side voice, never taking her eyes from the little girl.

"Not that I can recall."

"What are you?" Nathara addressed Jessica with curiosity and only mild trepidation. I hadn't caught on yet, so I kept looking around for the Bo Peep.

"Was it you the woman took? The one dressed up as a Little Bo Peep in black?" I asked her instead.

Right before our eyes, Jessica went from a little girl to the Little Bo Peep character, complete with a whimpering little girl. Then she morphed into a beleaguered mother holding a cooing baby. And finally, she returned to the tiny child, Jessica, or whatever the heck she was. I opened my mouth to ask what was going on when Jessica transformed one more time, and this transformation left no doubt about what we were dealing with.

Despite having never seen one before in my lifetime, I knew I was standing before a dark fae in an instant. Her skin was dark grayish-brown like weathered wood, and her hair was silver. Then, peering into otherworldly eyes that were golden and phosphorous, I shuddered as the total weight of this creature's malevolence hit me.

"Margaret Fortune."

The dark fae's voice had the ancient sound of something eons old and removed from use, as if an old door pried open after a long time closed and rusted were suddenly thrown open by force—jarring and unusual.

"Who are you? What did you do with Jessica? With the other child you stole?"

I heard a scraping sound like rocks tumbling into a tight chasm only to realize the being was laughing at me.

"Well, that's creepy," said Nathara.

Oh? Do you think?

"There is no stolen child. 'Tis but a glamor to trick the eyes—and methinks I've succeeded. As for Jessica, she is no longer. At one time, we were playmates, a cherished friend. Until I needed to feed...and took her as my host. Her kind is food to the Danu, these lycanthropes. Too old am I to walk among the Breed without a youthful being to support my aged bones and help me to sustain my life. And lycanthropes are strong, serving my purpose."

"She sounds like a swell parasite, don't you think?" asked Nathara drolly.

"Hmm...yes. Delightful. Imagine playing with one's food until it was dinnertime?"

"I did not eat her. I use her to hunt among her kind. It is easy to fool them with one of their own as bait."

I felt my stomach lurch and I grew angry that this evil woman felt such apathy toward others.

"You haven't answered me, however. Other than being a dark fae, who are you, and what do you want?"

"Dark fae! You give us this name. Light, dark, there is no difference among my people! We are the Danu. We do not respond to fae."

"OK. So why does someone of the Danu know my name?" I asked boldly, trying not to cringe as the tall being loomed over me in her fury.

"I made the mistake of trifling awhile with a man, half-human, half-shifter. He was an interesting man from across the ocean. He called himself a Kitsune. Our dalliance produced a fanciful child—a crossbreed bastard my people would not accept. I would have killed my offspring, but for the fact he was quite a delightful beast. Easy to laugh, pleasant on the eyes, and useful as he grew older. I grew weary of my male paramour, plus he became enamored of my sister, so she and I dispatched him without further ado and made a tasty snack of him when the child was but four."

How delightful. This asshat gave a new spin to the Tereus, Procne, and Philomela story in Greek mythology.

"My people are sympathetic to these Kitsune as we have similarities and a common ancestral link long forgotten by the passage of time. Therefore, I consider them brethren and choose from among them for a host. This gave me free rein to hunt alongside them and occasionally feed when the need arose."

"Feed? You ate them?"

"It is my right. But moreover, I collect their skin. This is because my people require it. I never used to be this... evil. Although I do not consider myself so. But even among my kind, the consensus is I let the beast within me take hold. But those among my kind who feel so do not collect as I do. They will never understand the craving. The hunger. Nor do they complain when I bring them the skin of my victims."

Imagine feeling kinship with someone yet justified to make them a tasty snack on occasion. And what kind of evil were these fae, to let one of their own kind go so foul just for the skin of victims? What was that all about? Did they require it for survival? Or was this something trivial they decided they wanted, despite the horror of it all?

"So, this half-breed lover of yours...he only gave you one child?" Nathara asked.

"Yes. My offspring has characteristics of the Kitsune people, the Danu, and humans. But when he transforms, he is something to behold."

"And what does he transform into?" asked Nathara.

"What you in this realm call a fox."

Fox! It can't be. It would be too much of a coincidence.

My disgust with this woman and her bastard son had no bounds. I wanted to strike her dead now despite the many questions I still had but chose to hold back my wrath—for the time being.

"Florin Vulpe is your son." It was a statement, and I didn't wait for her to respond. "He is the one who performed that foul magic on my sister and turned her into a revenant. Why? Why come after my family?"

"Just one side of your family. I seek to wipe out every last one of you if I get the chance. But we Danu do so love to play with our dinner. It makes the meal all the more enjoyable."

"What did we ever do to you? And why should my sister and I be guilty by association?" I asked.

"Not all of your family. The Romanian side. Sins of the father and all. Is that not a common saying? Or, in this case...your mother. She is no longer. However, ask your father what she and her kind did to my people. There lies your answer. Now I am weary and must leave, but not before doing what I came here for."

I channeled my magic, as did Nathara as we stood back-to-back. While we enjoyed this little conversation, the werewolves had finally caught up to us. Nathara had her eyes on them while protecting my back, and I kept mine on the dark fae.

What? We might not like each other much, but she was one of my team, and I would fight to the death to protect one of my own. Nathara felt likewise.

"She's going to do something, Maggie. Don't take your eyes off her. I have this bunch."

I let my magic flare and watched amusement flicker across the face of the fae.

"You misunderstand. It is not you that I came for this

day—not yet. I hunger still but will depart and not hunt as I usually do. You will not see Jessica again, for she failed me, and I will dine on what's left of her. It seems I need new lycanthrope packs far from here to amuse myself. This one shall know of me, and I will not have an easy time of it. I so wish young Benji was still alive. He served me well."

My eyes widened at this news, and I fully comprehended how long a reign of terror this evil monster had among the werewolf packs in the area. Taking a few steps away from where Nathara and I stood poised, the dark fae continued.

"Yes, you are safe for now. Nor can I harm your sister, for she is exactly where we want her. I orchestrated this entire affair to study your group and learn your weaknesses. You are formidable. I will give you that. But you have a weakness for one in your group, and this will be your downfall. For he possesses something I seek."

My alarm bells were going off, and I raised my hands, preparing for the worst, only it came as words—not the physical attack I'd expected.

"You cannot best me, foolish one. Know this. I will bide my time. When your vampire lover gets you with child, only then shall you see me again. That is what I seek from you, Margaret Fortune. I want your child, a dark witch that possesses your keen psychic abilities mixed with the vampire. Only then will I give you the anecdote to return your sister to this side of the veil. Despite what others have told you, no magic exists but mine that can bring her back."

I shook my head in denial even as the dark fae began to chuckle.

"Oh, yes. Margaret Fortune. What I say will be. For even now, as every passing day goes by, so does another molecule of dear Ellie. Until someday, she will exist as pure thought, only to float endlessly alone, aware, with no rest, and with no one to interact. Then she will go mad and fade into the ether. Would you do this to your sister? Over a child, you'd barely know? Or will you obey those that are superior in every way and give me what I seek? Only time will tell."

The dark fae rose into the air in a swirl of smoke and magic, giving me a parting shot that left me trembling with fear.

"Or will you watch with every passing day the end of your sister that you hold so dear? Time is of the essence, Margaret Fortune. It seems yours is running out."

And with a large flash, the fae exploded with a crack like thunder—out of this plane to another. Where could she have gone?

The werewolves all fell back, confused and wary, and who could blame them? They began scenting the air, and I could tell they comprehended that Jessica was no longer among them. They were right, I was, well, perhaps not wrong...but certainly misguided by that heinous creature. The horror of her words finally registered with me, and I began to shake.

"Steady woman. We have time yet. And despite her dire prediction, it's her word against Caliente and that Samantha Geist. We'll get Ellie back—and spare any baby fangster you and Tor might have." Nathara placed her hand on my shoulder and squeezed. Her kindness alone gave me a fraction of the strength I needed to get through the rest of this night.

I only hoped in the coming days I could draw on others' strength as well.

I had a feeling I'd need to.

CHAPTER 15

With no kidnapped child, the dark fae and her ruse causing untold trauma to the families who'd borne witness to her treachery, the festival wound down to a dull roar until the last of the families had departed. Still quite a successful event, despite the horrible distraction.

Charity broke down when I explained what had transpired all those years ago, freeing Johnny from suspicion in doing so, and they spent the rest of the night and well into the next day trying to mend fences, at least among close family. I don't think the other packs in the area had the patience for explanations beyond what they'd already heard, so harrowing was the disclosure that for decades they'd been nothing more than prey to a dark fae.

Two days after Halloween, we found ourselves preparing to move on to our next stop...New Orleans. I didn't even bother wondering if something else would pop up and bring evil along with it. New Orleans and evil went hand and hand, and so did the fun. There was always a good time to be had in the Big Easy.

"Tomorrow we're on the road, and I for one, can't wait to see the end of this place," said Bella with a sigh. "Not that I won't enjoy being here next year. I'm just over howling furballs and all their pack drama."

"I'm just glad none of them flipped their switch. Can you imagine the horror of dealing with that dark fae and having howling, frenzied werewolves chomping at our heels?" sniffed Nathara. She was back to her pouty self, and even Sven couldn't bring a smile to her lips, even though he'd been trying for the last half hour.

"Well, I love New Orleans...and so does my sister. Right, Serena? We shall have a wondrous time down there." Sydney stretched then looked at me with a frown. "Hey... who's that tall blond speaking with Johnny? She looks familiar, and I... oh, oh noooo!"

Johnny came loping over to our picnic area, followed by none other than Pandora, the crossroads demon friend of my cousin Lily.

"Hiya, everyone. How're things?" Pandora looked like a slutty cheerleader on a bender. A teeny-tiny poodle skirt and even tighter sweater that didn't leave much to the imagination and showed off her assets, thigh-high boots with stiletto heels, and a belly button ring completed the ensemble. She even had two mini pom-pom hair scrunches holding her locks in identical pigtails. Dorie was a gum-popping menace!

The only one in our group who was even remotely excited to see Pandora was Ellie, who came flying over and embraced the demon in a ghostly bear hug. I was surprised to see they could make contact—wonders never ceased.

"Hey, Pandora. What brings you here?" I was almost afraid to hear her response.

"Oh, nothing. I just had some little things to take care of and sniffed the air, recognizing the scent of uptight succubae and an earthy elemental nearby, and thought I'd say howdy."

Serena and Sydney were already growling, but Bella stood and began to hiss upon hearing those words.

"I can't stay long. Um...or at all. But I did want to see Ellie and give her a gift."

"Oh! You are too sweet, Dorie! What did you bring me?" squealed Ellie. And really, my sister has had so much trauma in her life. I couldn't begrudge her some time with her new friend.

"Let's go in your RV, and I will show you. Unfortunately, it seems the company out here is a tad frosty."

Ellie and Dorie ran to my RV, and I let them go. I mean, how much harm could one crossroads demon do to a ghost? So I figured Ellie was fine. Better to separate the demon from my three friends, who began twitching in unison.

"Ladies. Not now. We've had enough trouble to last us a year. Leave Pandora be. She's here to see Ellie and no more."

Grumbling, the three acquiesced and took their seats once more.

"Hey! What about the Ouija board? Have you had time to examine it yet?" asked Sven, who'd joined Nathara at the picnic table and had his arm around her shoulder.

"No! I was going to wait until we had free time, but things have been...well..."

I trailed off, horrified to find myself blinking away tears with a lump lodged in my throat. I'd told no one what the dark fae commanded of me and swore Nathara to secrecy lest she gets it into her head to tell Tor. The last thing I wanted was to burden him with something I had no intention of going through. There was no way I'd ever have a child and give it up to that demented fae!

"Why don't you go get it now? Let's take a look inside and see if there is a treasure map! After all, that could be one reason the dark fae hit us with so many distractions—to keep you from finding the Ouija board," said Dara, clueless as to the real reason the fae came and taunted me.

"OK."

Leaving my seat, I hurried over to my RV. I scrambled inside to find Ellie and Pandora giggling over some items...all looked reasonably harmless, so I didn't pause to concern myself with whatever they were doing.

By the time I made it back to the picnic area, my friends cleared a spot on the table, and that's where I placed the old Ouija board—in exceptional condition for its age. Dara held up the key and handed it to Bella, who had her hand outstretched. I nodded, indicating she should do the honors and open it.

After a bit of scrutiny, Bella located the keyhole, and I remained breathless by Tor's side as she turned the lock, and we all heard a satisfying click.

A drawer slid open, and inside was a folded piece of yellowed paper and something sparkling.

"Oh, look! An emerald. Isn't it lovely?" Sydney reached over and lifted the gem hanging on a silver box chain that might be white gold and held it up to catch the light. Instantly, we could all sense magic coming from the item.

I pulled the paper out of the drawer and carefully unfolded it on the table's flat surface.

"What is it? A map?" asked Bella.

"I'm not sure," I said slowly, confused at everything written and drawn on the map of sorts.

Antoine stood and came to examine the item up close.

"That's not a normal map. It's a treasure hunt. Look at the diagram, and here, this smaller piece of paper has instructions on it. Follow the instruction and find the treasure—or whatever lies at the end marked by an 'X.' This is odd."

"Odd? It's exciting!" squealed Bella. "I love a good treasure hunt. Where does the 'X' mark the spot?"

I looked down at the paper, then up, where my eyes met Tor's, who instantly knew I was upset.

"What is it, lass?"

"You know how I told you the other day I didn't like coincidences?"

"Aye. Who does in this lot?"

"Well, this is either one huge coincidence, or we've been played."

"How so?" Antoine leaned down and cursed when he read the location marked on the paper.

"New Orleans." Antoine straightened once more and turned to me.

"Yes. New Orleans. And we just happen to be heading there next. So, what are the odds of having this Ouija board wind up being sold to farmers down here in Texas, meeting up with that evil fae creature, then having our next stop be the exact place we need to go to solve this puzzle?"

"Well, I don't know about you, but I'm up for a treasure hunt. Especially if it means bringing us closer to ending that fae and her promise of..."

"Ahem. Nathara. While I appreciate you wanting to capture the fae, we have to tread lightly. We still don't know her game plan. I'm sure she will turn up when we least expect it again and taunt us with more of her miserable machinations. For now, we have to make copies of this map and pass them out to everyone. I need you to work on this on the way down to New Orleans so we can play it out and find out what manner of mischief is coming next."

I didn't entirely use that exact word, but the sentiment is the same.

Johnny was all smiles, and his tale and the resolution of the ill will between his family was the only good thing to come out of this mess. My heart was happy for him even as it ached for mine and Tor's future...or nonfuture as it were.

"Well, New Orleans is never dull. We should get some good sleep tonight, turn in early, and be ready for anything in the morning." Dara, ever the optimist, was probably the most excited, seeing as how she restocked many of her woo-woo potions and fortune-telling items in that lively city.

Everyone scattered then to do their packing and preparations, except for Johnny, Serena, and Sydney. They had the task of taking his and Tor's RV to the dumping station and cleaning out the water tanks. The rest of our vehicles were already completed and awaiting tomorrow's departure.

Tor looked over at me and smiled gently. "Who's keeping secrets now, lass?"

How he could tell something was troubling me was bothersome, but I didn't know how to discuss the horrible decree the dark fae hit me with, so I tried to deflect with humor.

"Tell me your secrets, and I'll tell you mine."

Sighing loudly, Tor stood and gave me a peck on the cheek, then pulled me to my feet and thoroughly kissed me despite Antoine sitting three feet away.

"When you're ready then." Turning to Antoine, Tor said, "I'm going to tell the drivers to head out and make sure they have all the coordinates and such. Nathara is with Estelle doing her end of things. Do you need anything else from me?"

"No. Thanks for taking care of the truckers. I'll see you in the morning."

When Tor departed, Antoine gave me a weighted look that spoke volumes. "Tor is right. You are keeping something from us." I went to protest, but Antoine held up his hand to stop me. "Mags, I won't get in your business. But know this. If you have anything that involves you or any team member, we should all be aware of it and work together. That's what being a team is all about. OK?"

I nodded yes, not entirely having a voice to answer his query and agree with his statement.

"Funny with that fae. We all thought her a werewolf and a child at that, but she turned out to be one in sheep's clothing. Or, in her case, a dark and foul creature, warped and twisted. I don't want you fighting any battle alone. Do you understand?"

"I've got it, boss."

Antoine chuckled at my insistence upon calling him that.

"This fae has ties to Florin Vulpe. And we know what he did. I'm just not sure where it's all leading. Until we discover what their plans are, stay vigilant—not that I have to tell you any of this."

"Thanks, Antoine. For everything. For being my friend and for, well...everything," I ended lamely.

I watched as Ellie and Pandora left my RV and ran toward Sydney and Serena's, then disappeared around the back side of it. Those two were as thick as thieves, and I wondered at Pandora's sudden appearance.

With nothing left to do but get my things in order, I said goodnight to Antoine and went to feed Bob.

～

"What is going on with those two? I swear, ever since we headed out this morning, Serena has been driving erratically. Try the CB again and if that doesn't work, try getting Sydney on her cell phone." I didn't like how the succubae were driving and was worried enough to call Antoine following behind me with Dara. Johnny and Tor were behind Antoine, leaving me, Bella, and Ellie following Sven and Nathara, Serena and Sydney leading the way.

"Mags, are you seeing this?"

My CB crackled, and Sven's voice came over the speakers.

"Roger, that. What do you think is wrong with them?"

I heard Ellie snicker softly and became instantly suspicious. Turning to glance her way, I witnessed her face transform from one filled with delight to affected innocence, and she didn't fool me one bit.

"Ellie! What is it! What did you do?"

Suddenly my cell phone rang, and I saw it was Sydney calling.

"Maggie Fortune! I am going to kill that sister of yours even if she is a flipping ghost!"

"Sydney, what's wrong? Why is Serena driving so wild?"

"What's wrong? What's wrong! Ask your foolhardy sibling what's wrong! She and that demon friend must have cursed us or spelled the RV. Everything is going wonky and... wait...is that? Oh no. I just saw a pixie fly by and....argh! I'm going to kill that Pandora! Just you wait!"

Ellie couldn't contain her laughter any longer, and I rolled my eyes.

Great.

The last thing we needed was a pixie problem.

Hopefully, it's just one harmless little guy like the one

we'd left in Sweet Briar, Georgia. Unless perhaps it's the same one. We'd magically transported the few we discovered in those old games the vampire brought. So, it couldn't be those causing mischief. Either way, I'm sure we could send the little imp back to where he came from, and that would restore peace and tranquility.

After all, we had bigger things to worry about in the Big Easy. No time for pixies!

Right?

∼

Thank you for reading! I hope you enjoyed this latest installment.

There is only ONE way I am ever going to attain world dominance and become a best-selling paranormal mystery and romance author. I need your reviews! Won't you please help me achieve my goals? Reviews mean *everything* to an author; it allows others who may not have heard of me yet take a chance on one of my tales. Amazon, Goodreads, and BookBub are just a few places you can leave them. I hope you consider taking the time to write one for me—and again, I thank you!

I hope you loved meeting Maggie, Ellie, and the rest of the characters. The next book in the Fortune-Telling Twins series, A Pocketful of Pixies, is coming soon! New Orleans is calling and a treasure hunt to end all treasure hunts will be on the agenda. Will Maggie and her team find out what the cryptic map is leading to, or will they run into one obstacle after another with the chase ending in frustration, and worse, finding no more clues on how to help Ellie and stop her from fading into nothingness?

And if you enjoyed A Werewolf in Sheep's Clothing you'll love reading about Maggie and Ellie's cousin, Lily Sweet, a naïve dark witch who discovers her powers and reunites with a family she never knew while coming to terms with her topsy-turvy magical ability. Home Sweet Witch is Book 1 of The Lily Sweet Mysteries and is FREE on Kindle Unlimited!

"Excellent."

- Butterfly & Birch Reviews.

For a dose of steamy paranormal romance, check out Tarni Vanderzee's story...Lily's siren friend, in my new series, Secret Sirens. The first book is Siren Rise. It's a tale with romance, mystery, and suspense that goes over Tarni's life from eighteen onwards as she tries to defy the conformity and misogyny among the sirens and live among humans while seeking out fame, fortune, and power. Enough power to overthrow those that rule the siren world. Only something gets in her way. An up-and-coming rock star named Logan MacDuff who has secrets of his own, the kind that might get Tarni into deep water...deeper than even she can withstand.

READ SIREN RISE here!

I'd appreciate your help in spreading the word, including telling friends and family. Reviews help readers find books! Please leave a review on your favorite book site.

You can also join my Facebook Group: Author Bettina M. Johnson's Team Wicked for exclusive giveaways and sneak peeks of future books—and just plain silliness!

SIGN UP FOR BETTINA M. JOHNSON'S NEWSLETTER: http://eepurl.com/gZKo51

∼

I write in my own style that may not be everyone's cup of tea—so if you enjoy my characters and humor, my plots, how the storyline is developing, etc. and are eagerly anticipating the next in the series, be aware that I am just as excited as you are—I've found someone who thinks my story ideas are neat! That is thrilling for any writer to know (or it should be). THANK YOU!

Visit my official website to receive updates, find out about special offers and new releases, or read my blog about writing and farm life - complete with photos - you might even catch me mowing my ten acres (seriously): http://www.bettinamjohnson.net

For more information or to contact me:
author@bettinamjohnson.net

For even more (if you just can't enough of me) follow my Social Media Links

Mailing List - https://bit.ly/2BvQXmP
BookBub - https://bit.ly/2Epejwj
Goodreads - https://bit.ly/3aTejQW
Author Page - Amazon - https://amzn.to/3lj7L2L
Instagram - https://bit.ly/2QpZao1

TikTok - https://bit.ly/2PQa6Hg
MeWe - https://bit.ly/36A2RcM
Facebook - https://bit.ly/3gOaFZY
Twitter: https://bit.ly/3jahMgY
YouTube - https://bit.ly/2Stvy2X

SOCIAL MEDIA LINKS

I write in my own style that may not be everyone's cup of tea—so if you enjoy my characters and humor, my plots, how the storyline is developing, etc. and are eagerly anticipating the next in the series, be aware that I am just as excited as you are—I've found someone who thinks my story ideas are neat! That is thrilling for any writer to know (or it should be). THANK YOU!

Visit my official website to receive updates, find out about special offers and new releases, or read my blog about writing and farm life - complete with photos - you might even catch me mowing my ten acres (seriously): http://www.bettinamjohnson.net

For more information or to contact me:
author@bettinamjohnson.net

For even more (if you just can't enough of me) follow my Social Media Links

SOCIAL MEDIA LINKS

Mailing List - https://bit.ly/2BvQXmP
BookBub - https://bit.ly/2Epejwj
Goodreads - https://bit.ly/3aTejQW
Author Page - Amazon - https://amzn.to/3lj7L2L
Instagram - https://bit.ly/2QpZao1
TikTok - https://bit.ly/2PQa6Hg
MeWe - https://bit.ly/36A2RcM
Facebook - https://bit.ly/3gOaFZY
Twitter: https://bit.ly/3jahMgY
YouTube - https://bit.ly/2Stvy2X

ABOUT THE AUTHOR

I always knew I wanted to write. As a kid, way before the technology age had hit, I'd be stuck in the car with the folks as we drove from our home on Staten Island, NY, where I was born and raised, to our family property in the Catskill Mountains. To drive away boredom, I would sit, staring out the window, and create adventures of daring thieves riding horseback along the road, trying to escape the law. Other times I'd imagine a wild girl riding her unicorn into battle (I had a vivid imagination - we didn't have video games yet!).

As the years passed, I'd start writing a book, then stop, then start again only to let life get in the way, until one day I had an epiphany—a kick in the pants moment. If I waited any longer, all those wonderful characters in my head would never have their stories told, and that made me sad. So, I treated writing as my career. Once I started, it became apparent nothing would ever stop me again. YOU, dear reader, are stuck with me until I go off to that great library in the sky...or wherever writers go when they crumble to dust in front of their typewriters (or laptops...whatever!).

I live in the North Georgia mountains on what I like to call a farm, with my husband and almost adult kids, a Cairn Terrier, three cats, and fish. Occasionally other critters show up to keep things exciting.

BOOKS BY BETTINA M. JOHNSON

The Lily Sweet Mysteries:

Home Sweet Witch
Witch Way is Up?
How To Train Your Witch
Sweet Home Liliana
Witch Way Did He Go?
Revenge is Sweet, Witch
Witch and Peace
The Sweet Spell of Success
I Spell Trouble
Sweet Briar Witch (Coming Soon)

∾

The Fortune-Telling Twins Mysteries:

A Tale of Two Sisters
Double Toil and Trouble
Fire and Earth, Sisters at Birth
Kindred Spirits
A Djinn and Tonic
A Werewolf in Sheep's Clothing
A Pocketful of Pixies (Coming Soon)

Secret Sirens:

Siren Rise

Siren Star (Coming Soon)

Made in United States
North Haven, CT
30 October 2022